Is it Love or Infatuation

What do you say?

A novel by

Devi Vinayagam

Become
Shakespeare
.com

First published by 2017

Becomeshakspeare.com
Wordit Content De sign & Editing Services Pvt Ltd
Unit - 26, Building A -1, Nr Wadala RTO,
Wadala (East), Mumbai 400037, India
T: +91 8080226699
Wordit Art Fund helps deserving authors publish their work by
providing monetary support. To apply for funding, please visit us
atwww.BecomeShakespeare.com

©

ISBN - 978-93-86487-79-7

Dedication

To my beloved parents, who educated me and enabled me to reach this level.

To all my teachers and mentors for their support and guidance.

To my siblings, for their unending support as well guidance in authoring this book.

My college friends and classmates.

Of course for an interesting girl, I met in a bus journey. And without her this book would not be possible. You are such an amazing person as well a good friend of mine.

To all my readers, who walk and read at the same time.

And to me who used to think, what I didn't know would fill a book. Well, here it is!

Acknowledgement

First and foremost, I would like to thank the Almighty. After writing this book, I realized how blessed I am to have the gift of writing. Again, I thank almighty, for giving me the power to follow my passions as well to pursue my dreams.

Next, I would like to thank my parents and siblings for standing beside me throughout my career and for allowing me to follow my ambitions. I hoped that one day they can read this book and understand why I spent so much time in front of my computer and my hope is fulfilled now.

Thanks to all my college mates as well friends, especially the friends whom I met during my bus journeys. If I didn't get a chance to meet you all, I would not have written this book.

I would really like to thank the entire team of Lead start publications and Become Shakespeare for providing me the opportunity to become the author of this book. This work would not have been possible without the supports of the Word it art fund of Become Shakespeare as well Lead start publications and I am grateful for them. Also, I am grateful to all of those with whom I have had the pleasure to work with during this book.

There have been many people who have walked alongside with me in my years of life journey. They have guided me, placed opportunities in front of me and showed me the doors that might be useful to open. I would like to thank each and every one of them.

Finally, nobody has been more important to me in the pursuit of this book than the members of my family. My family has always supported me in authoring this book and I really appreciate it. I would like to thank my parents once again, whose love and guidance are with me in whatever I pursue. They are the ultimate role models. Most importantly, once again, I wish to thank my loving and supportive siblings, who provide unending inspiration.

Prologue

Bangalore!! Bangalore!! Bangalore!!

Yes!! Finally, I could see a Chennai to Bangalore semi sleeper bus, entering the Vellore bus terminal.

I rushed towards the bus conductor and asked; is there a seat to Bangalore. After checking the already booked seats list of that bus, the conductor said; yes, you can go and sit in seat number 11.It was a window seat. Okay, I said and got into the bus.

My seat partner was sitting on my seat. Hi this seat is mine, can I have it please.

Oh! Sure, she said with a cute smile on her face. Finally, I was on my seat. The bus started its journey. We both were seeing outside the window. Though it takes approximately 5 hours to Bangalore from Vellore by bus, at what time we will be there in Bangalore? I enquired my seat partner.

About 9 pm we will be there, if there is no traffic jam after Hosur and near electronic city. After 15 minutes, she asked a question. What is your name?

Roopika Sivanathan.

What is your name?

Deeksha, Deeksha Karthikeyan. Are you working in Bangalore Roopika? Yes, working in a drug research Company, but basically I am a Physiotherapist, completed my UG in Chennai and PG in Bangalore.

Oh! Wow! Even I am a physiotherapist, working in a drug research company, but in Mumbai, completed my UG in Bangalore and PG in Mumbai. I am going to Bangalore, just to attend one of my college friends' wedding, Deeksha said.

Deeksha, I think you are great in studies? I asked. No, Roopika it's nothing like that. Deeksha, am I disturbing you? If you want to sleep and have some rest, you can. No, I was at ease with you and I too adore these moments, Deeksha said. She, never slumbered while travelling. Thus, I asked her to tell something about her friends, boyfriend and college life. But only if she thinks she was okay with sharing her story with me, then please do. I would love to hear it, I said.

Why not? Roopika. I am missing all my college days and friends, after meeting you Roopika. So, let me tell you.

As we went on with our bus journey, Deeksha started to wind back her life from her college days.

Chapter 1

September 05 2005 it was my (this Deeksha's) first day in college.

My wish was to join a college in Chennai city as I was from a small town nearby to Chennai. But I was surprised when I got admittance into a college in Bangalore. So it looked like a dream for me when I stepped into such a beautiful university campus in Bangalore with my dad, with lots of expectations about my career and life ahead.

On the way to my department I could see students almost from all states of India except a very few in that university campus. I suddenly stopped at the entrance of a classroom as my dad asked me to. At that point in time I realized it was not a dream, however, I was standing outside my 1st year classroom of Physiotherapy department with my dad.

I kept my entire luggage down. And I could see only a few students sitting inside that classroom and a professor were coming out of that classroom to greet us.

The professor entered my name in the first year attendance register. The professor told the college reopened that day and more students are yet to join them in the upcoming days of that week. Hence, classes are not started yet. Consequently, the professor asked me to finish my hostel formalities first and to join them back in the classroom. As my whole day went with hostel formalities, I was about to join my class the next day.

Everything looked new to me, new Malayalee roommates, new faces, new life!!

The next day morning before leaving for college, I just stood outside my room in college hostel 1st floor for a few minutes. I was astonished when I heard my name being called by someone. When I started searching for that girl, again I heard a blaring tone which asked me to see up towards 3rd floor.

Yes, I could see a North Indian girl in 3rd floor waving her hands towards me. Once I saw her, she screamed again. Hey, you are Deeksha right? I nodded my head in approval. I am Anusha your classmate. I saw you yesterday with your dad in our department. Just give me five minutes I will come down and let's go together to college. I just nodded my head again.

Then it was me, Anusha and Manasa my North Indian classmates who were in hostel food court which was a common food court to have breakfast and lunch for the whole university hostel boys and girls. We had our breakfast and started walking towards our department.

On our way we met a few of our south Indian classmates and that was none other than Malvika and Vinodhini.

Anusha introduced me to both of my south Indian classmates. As soon as I saw my south Indian classmates on the way to our department I realized, I was not in north India though I have not reached my classroom yet.

Also, Anusha introduced me to all my batch mates after we reached our classroom. Exactly after a week I could see so many new faces in my classroom, whereas it looked like all the first year students of Physiotherapy department had came down from their hometowns.

Yes, eventually it was a total of 43 students in the first year Physiotherapy department. Among that majority of them were girls.

As the days flew by I got a new friend from my batch. She was none other than Malvika. It was just a pleasant Monday morning where I and Malvika were chit chatting with each other in our classroom. Suddenly our batch could hear from one of our Professors that our classroom has been shifted next to our department staff room. Moreover, the professor asked all of us to move to our new classroom immediately.

I speculated after hearing it as I was a late admission student. So Malvika said; Deeksha our classrooms were shifted as because our first year batch was ragged by our whole physiotherapy department seniors at a time, i.e., from immediate seniors up to the final years of Physiotherapy department and one of our classmates a Malayalee student from our batch had lost his smart phone on that day. Therefore, we complained to college management regarding mobile theft and ragging by seniors. Hence, strict warning was given to seniors of the whole Physiotherapy department by the college management and at the same time holidays were given to first years immediately for around 2 weeks from that day. Hence, the college had reopened then, after those holidays. For this reason, our classroom was shifted next to the staff room. After hearing that, I said; oh ok Malvika. Anyhow, come; let's move to our new classroom as all our classmates had already started moving.

Of course, then it was desk allocation time in a new classroom and out of 4 rows, two rows have been allotted for boys and vice versa.

Malvika and I occupied first desk in a row allotted for boys due to unavailability of empty desks in girl's rows and boys occupied from next desk onward. So it was Jack, Divakar and Prakash, who sat next to our desk.

Introduction between us started just with a simple Hi. And by that time I never ever expected or never knew that Jack was going to be my special someone in my life with whom I would wish to spend the rest of my life.

Slowly, after 2 weeks our most anticipated first year classes started. Next to that week or two, I moved out of my college hostel as I didn't like my hostel food. I stayed in a separate house for rent which was near to my cousin home, also which was walk able distance from my college. And I started bringing lunch to college from my cousin home daily.

Really, it was enjoyable days for me with all the new faces and for all of a sudden, on one fine day I got a gang of new friends from my batch.

Malvika who was my friend by that time, got one more new friend, apart from me, from the final year of Physiotherapy department and she was none other than our senior Ruvina.

Malvika slowly started having lunch with our senior and I was left alone. Few of my classmates asked me repeatedly to join them for lunch as I used to have my lunch alone. I hesitated to join them for lunch at the beginning. Then after some days I joined them as per their request. But at that moment none of us expected that we all have gone to turn as good friends forever.

Slowly the first year students had fallen themselves into 5 gangs. Among those 5, our gang was a big one which had 12 people altogether and we had Jack, Divakar and Prakash in our gang. I am the one who introduced Jack to my gang.

My friends list includes Meenu, Lalitha, Deepika, Sayina, Shamili, Sonia, Sobia, Somesh, Kiran and the above mentioned three guys. Slowly we become familiar with each other in the gang.

After every class our gang always had short chat with each other regarding our previous session held in college and also altogether we had so much of fun. As days passed by myself and Jack became good friends.

Everyone in our group felt true friendship is rare these days and we all have been lucky to have met and made friends with people whom we can trust blindly. We all were having awesome days in college altogether. We all believed life without friends is like the world without colour. Also, each one of us felt our friendship bond was extremely special and unique in its own way. It was really amazing days of our college life.

Canteen became our regular hangouts. We started sharing our food daily. It was a new world altogether. And we all loved each moment of it. Above all we bonded with each other quickly.

I never knew that Jack knows Tamil as I thought Jack was a North Indian Christian, later I came to know through my friend Lalitha that Jack was a south Indian Christian (Tamilian) and his family got settled in North India as Jack parents were working over there. So he could speak Tamil and Jack didn't say it out because of ragging, as our seniors would rag more if Jack knows our language.

Slowly, as the weeks flew by I felt from heart that Jack was the type of person whom I was looking for. Once Again, I asked myself, was he the one I am looking for? My heart said, yes! I need that care, affection, friendship and love from Jack for lifetime that's until I am alive in this beautiful world.

Jack looked smart enough, he always had a good sense of humor as well as his dressing sense and hairstyle looked good too. Everyone who saw him could say yes, he was a north Indian but in reality that's not the case.

Physiotherapy department also had a leisure hour after each session that's between different sessions as because our professors always said whatever they teach had to be understood clearly by the students because after finishing our courses we are going to treat human beings. So probably we never had classes immediately after lunch as most of us felt sleepy. Withal, in leisure hours we had lots and lots of fun always.

On a witty day in college when everyone was chit chatting and having fun with their friends in a classroom, we were unable to find Jack in his desk or somewhere around our friends. Finally, I find him sitting alone at the last desk of classroom reading a diary and all our friends decided not to disturb him as the diary looked like his personal diary. After a few minutes, Jack himself, came back to his desk with his diary. By the time almost all our friends went out of the classroom for a small break. Only very few were in class and I was one among them.

After a couple of minutes of Jack advent, I gradually started asking Jack, was it your personal diary? Do you have a habit of writing a diary? Jack kept quiet for some time and then he said yes!!

My wish was to know utterly about Jack, but I never knew what Jack felt about me. So I was scared whether something will go wrong if I go ahead and ask for his personal diary. After a long wait, I gathered my valor and asked; Jack, could you give me your personal diary to read? No, it's my personal, and I won't, Jack said. I was upset after hearing it because I never anticipated those words from Jack.

Usually Sayina, Jack and myself would leave together to home as most of our friends leave through college back gates as those routes were a shortcut to their homes while we 3 among our gang leave through the front gate of the University campus as Jack Hostel which was inside the college premises was on the way to the university front gate and Sayina bus stop was also on the way to my room.

When classes were over for that day as Sayina was on leave both myself and Jack started walking together. And I could see Jack carries his personal diary in one hand. When we both were near to his hostel, I solicited Jack once again to give his personal diary to me to read. Also, I promised I would hand over his diary back to him by next day morning in college. Though Jack kept quiet for a few seconds, for all of a sudden Jack gave his personal diary to me and he asked hey by tomorrow morning will you give it back for sure?!

I was so cheery and amazed. I could hear my mind voice, yeah, yes, Jack loves me!! Or else why Jack gave his personal diary to me to read. Then, within a few seconds when I came back to the real world, I realized that we both were near to the Jack hostel entrance. Further, I could see Jack staring at me for my reply. Then immediately I replied oh!! Hey, yes for sure Jack, I will return your personal diary back to you by tomorrow morning. Then we both bid bye to each other and left for home.

After reaching my room, as I finished my usual works, I started reading Jack personal diary. Then I came to know about Jack personally, his family, school life, his occasional drinking habits, especially his uncle scolding for that and finally his uncle words to him, that's First learn to earn money and stand on your own feet then indulge in all these things.

I understood Jack was somehow different from what I thought.

Yes, the next day morning the moment I saw Jack in our classroom, I just handed over his personal diary back to him with a grin on my face. By that time we both could see a small problem going on in our classroom between a few of our classmates regarding representative selection as our first year batch had one north Indian representative Anusha and one south Indian representative that was none other than my friend Divakar.

Our batch south Indians always had a small fight with our North Indians classmates as those North Indians students were dominating us, though they were very few in our batch and most of us were south Indians. Finally, after a long debate, we all ended it by selecting two south Indian representatives for our batch.

Besides all those I had a habit of writing my personal diary from my schooling. The next day, as I had leisure hours in college and as I didn't have time to write it at home, I bought my personal diary to college with the intention to pen down the yesterday happenings of my life or else I thought I will forget it.

As soon as our morning sessions were over for that day, everyone was chit chatting here and there in the classroom. Therefore, I started writing my diary, but I didn't expect that Jack would come and stand in front of me when I was about to finish penning down my yesterday happenings. I was afraid because I thought Jack would ask for my personal diary to read. Yes, unerringly the same happened.

I said no! Am sorry I don't want to give my personal diary to anyone, including you Jack, because it's very personal but inside my mind certain thoughts were flowing that's I don't want to give it to you because my personal diary contains about you too Jack that's why, the day I met you and how I felt and how I feel till now about you.

Also, I believed if Jack comes to know about it right then, it would be a problem and Jack won't accept it too, because Jack was a type of guy who always said love is different from infatuation. Also, Jack used to say, one should know the difference between infatuation and love. So I said to myself, please don't ask to me right now Jack.

After a few seconds when I came back to my senses, I realized that Jack waved his hands before my eyes and shouting like Hello!! Are you here, hope you are in a day dream...

I said no! Am not in a day dream!! Am here!!

Jack laughed and asked, oh!! Really?!!

Then after a small pause, Jack said; hey Deeksha anyhow, finally you came out of your dream world?!! So, anything interesting written down there in your diary?! If yes! Then I have to read it for sure, so give it to me now. I will read and give back to you before you leave for the day.

I said no way Jack! I couldn't.

Jack in turn asked so you could know about me personally, but I shouldn't right?

Then I am not your best friend right?

I was dumbfounded.

I could hear my mind voice again, anyway Deeksha your diary contains all your info from your school days and only at the end you had written about your college days. For sure Jack won't read about your college days as he would not have enough time to go through your school days alone and even if he starts reading randomly or from the end, it was not that easy to find that page where you had written about him. So you could give him your personal diary.

Finally, I gave my personal diary as I didn't have any other option.

Jack took it and went to the last desk of classroom which was always free and started to read. I looked around to see if someone else had seen us. But everyone was busy with the daily activities. So I breathed a sigh of relief.

Then, within few seconds I joined my friends, started chit chatting with them; also I had an eye on what Jack does. Approximately after one hour Jack came back to my desk and he gave my personal diary back to me. Unexpectedly, we both could hear Malvika's crying sound by that time. Hence, Jack asked me to go and convince her and he sat at my desk.

At last when the classes were over for that day and when we were about to leave for home, Jack said hey Deeksha C'mon pack up and call out Sayina (as we three among our gang always leave together to home) so that we could reach our homes earlier and one more request to you Deeksha before leaving. I just need your personal diary again. As I couldn't read it completely, I wish to take it with me today to the hostel. And I make sure I would return it back to you by tomorrow morning in college.

I did not know what to say. I thought it was impossible for Jack to go through the whole diary in one night. Therefore, I handed over my personal diary to Jack again. However, I asked Jack to return my personal diary by next day morning in college for sure. Also, I prayed to God; even if Jack reads my personal diary randomly he should never ever open up the page where I had written about him. Afterwards we both including our friend Sayina started leaving for home.

I never thought my destiny would be something different from my expectations.

In college, from next day onward, I could see a slight difference in Jack attitude towards me. I was much worried, but I was not pretty sure why Jack behaved to me in such a way. Whenever!! I was there with my friends Jack won't be there with us. Jack started avoiding me. I felt to know the exact reason for it. Also, I thought it's good to ask him straight away what his problem in talking to me was.

I went ahead and asked; Jack, what's your problem in talking to me?

Jack said; no I don't have any problem. I am the same Jack, only you think that I and my attitude have changed and he left the place immediately.

That minute suddenly something strikes my mind. Jack would have read my pages of college days in my personal diary and so. Might be Jack didn't love me. Hence, Jack started avoiding me, but I did not know how to confirm it. Also, I prayed to God, it shouldn't be that way because I loved Jack madly.

Then, when my friend Meenu asked me to give my personal diary, I was taken aback. She started asking; Deeksha, will you give it to Jack alone and not to me? She kept on asking; Jack was your only friend? Was it? Am not your friend?

Though I was astounded, certain queries arose in my mind that's oh God!! Was it my personal diary or what? Why the hell Jack went and said Meenu that he read my personal diary.

Meenu and Lalitha were my close friends among my gang and they both had never masked anything about their personal lives to me yet. For that reason, I said; ok Meenu I will bring my Personal diary tomorrow while coming to college, but you don't read it in college, because it's something personal. I hope you understood. Better you take home and bring it back the next day morning for college without fail Meenu. Yup, sure, Meenu said.

At the end of that day before leaving for home, I was just waiting for Meenu at the entrance of my classroom. Almost all my friends had already left for the day. And it seemed Jack was about to leave, as he was bidding bye to Meenu.

Though I saw Jack, I just kept quiet and waited for Meenu. When Jack came to classroom entrance, he just came to me and asked;

Deeksha did Meenu asked about your personal diary? I was annoyed as well bewildered and when I was about to reply him, we both could see Meenu rushing towards us from inside the classroom and she said; hey Jack, Deeksha told she will bring her diary tomorrow. Okay! Fine Meenu, Jack said and he left alone. Next Meenu went back to her desk and took all her notebooks and she said; Come Deeksha we will leave for the day. Then I remember thinking to myself; something was wrong; but let me wait and see what it was.

In college the next day morning I gave my personal diary to Meenu. After receiving it Meenu said she would give back my personal diary the next day morning without fail.

On the same day in college during our leisure hours I could see Meenu and Jack standing outside our classroom and speaking about something besides Meenu was having my personal diary in her hand. Conversely, I could see all my other friends' chit chatting in the classroom. Though I saw all those, I never interrupted nor raised any queries to Meenu or Jack.

I was just eagerly waiting for the next day to get back my personal diary from Meenu but I didn't expect Meenu would come and say that she want to speak a little to me before giving my diary back. And Meenu said; let's speak about it this afternoon Deeksha, during our leisure hour. I was irritated after hearing that and I was sure it was regarding love and Jack. So from Meenu conversation, again, I made sure that Jack had read my whole diary and now Jack knows that I love him.

I controlled my annoyance and said; okay Meenu lets speak about it in our leisure hours. At last, the most awaited leisure hours of that day had come and as a first year classroom was located on the first floor, Meenu took me to the second floor balcony as none of our classmates would be there except our seniors.

Meenu started saying, Deeksha don't feel execrable about what I am going to say. I was petite scared after hearing Meenu words. Furthermore, I instantly wanted to know what it was. So I asked

Meenu to convey it to me quickly regardless of whatever it might be.

Meenu said; I am really sorry to convey it. Jack doesn't love you and it seems he read your personal diary randomly in college on that day. Moreover, it looks like he read about your college days. So Jack came to know on that day itself that you love him. That's why Jack had asked for your personal diary on the same day again. And Jack had read your whole diary in his hostel on the same day night. Hence, Jack started avoiding you from the next day.

As I am your close friend, Jack bought it to my attention. Jack asked me to put it across to you Deeksha and as I didn't believe in what he said, Jack asked me to go through your personal diary and that's why I asked for your personal diary.

Meenu saw my reaction when she conveyed it. Suddenly we both could see Jack coming towards the second floor balcony. Once Jack came near me he asked hey Deeksha did Meenu say everything?!!

I just nodded my head and I was about to burst into tears. Hence, Meenu shouted at Jack. Please get back to the classroom and don't speak anything to her right now Jack. Thus, Jack left to the classroom instantaneously.

Then, within fraction of seconds tears rolled down my cheeks. I never want to get back to my classroom. I kept on crying and my eyes had become swollen. Unexpectedly, our next session (Anatomy session) which was the last session for that day has been canceled.

After a while, Meenu convinced me to an extent by some means, and we both were back to our classroom. I sat silently in my desk controlling my tears or else I thought everyone in the classroom would ask for it.

Although all my classmates were chit chatting here and there, at least one person from each group (as we had five gangs in classroom) came and asked me; Deeksha what happened to you? Why you are so silent and what happened to your eyes? Did you cry?!!

I said no, nothing like that, I am good. And I started helping one of my classmates to write his previous Psychology notes as he was on long leave to college in the past. But none of my friends came to convince me as Meenu said to every one of my friends about what happened. They all felt; it would take a few more days for me to accept it and to come back to normal life. So they don't want to make me cry more by convincing me.

At the end of that day when everyone started leaving to home Meenu came to my desk and said hey Deeksha I know you are feeling awful. But if you want to cry just cry out here and please don't cry after going to your room as there won't be anyone with you. I kept quiet for a few seconds, then I said bye to Meenu and left for the day.

The moment I reached my room I burst into tears like anything. I couldn't even imagine a life without Jack. I was crying and thinking again and again why Jack said like that.

The next day morning in college the whole first year batch was waiting outside our classroom as the classroom lock was not opened yet by our housekeeping personnel.

I was bound by my friends exception was Meenu. Meenu came in between and joined us. Slowly, after a few seconds Meenu started asking; Deeksha are you okay?! I just kept quiet. And she added; Deeksha, as we do have Christmas holidays for a week, you just go for a small trip to Trichy during the Christmas holidays with our friends Shamili and Sonia, as they both were going for a trip with their hostel friends. Shamili and Sonia had already booked a ticket for you too. So you join them for the trip, Meenu said.

After a small pause Meenu again added; I am sure!! You would feel much better after coming back from holidays. Next, Shamili and Sonia said the same to me. I kept quiet and I did not react to any of my friends. But I realized my friends' thoughts; they all looked forward to seeing their old friend Deeksha after that trip.

We had another half an hour left out for our classes to get started, so once our classrooms were opened Meenu and Shamili asked me to come with them to an STD booth (as none of the host élites and localities had mobiles) which was located just outside our college campus as Shamili want to inform her parents regarding Trichy trip. They both asked me to inform my parents as well about my Trichy trip as I won't be able to go home for Christmas holidays. Finally, I did the same.

In college, the next day afternoon after having lunch I stood silently in the first floor balcony along with a few of my classmates while all others were chit chatting. Suddenly Jack came that way and he gave chocolates to everyone over there except me. He said it was his brother's birthday that's why he was distributing chocolates.

At last Jack came and stood near me. He started whispering something slowly into my ears where no one could hear it except me.

Jack whispered I am really sorry Deeksha, if I had behaved to you in such a way that made you to feel like I love you? I don't have any thoughts like that. I thought you only as my friend.

It seemed Meenu came to balcony searching for me by the time and when she saw Jack next to me she came running towards us. As soon as Meenu reached us she bellowed at Jack. Jack get out of here and please don't talk anything to Deeksha as I conveyed already whatever you said to.

Meenu asked Jack to leave that place immediately. Jack said ok and left the place. Next, Meenu tapped my shoulder and asked me to come to the classroom.

I was hushed and I stood alone for a few more minutes there thinking why all these Jack words shouldn't be a dream? I kept on thinking why did we meet? Why did our friendship grow? Why did Jack give me his personal diary? Why? I don't know. I only know, Jack was the one who came and introduced himself to me. At that time, neither of us knew that within 3 months, I will fall in love with him.

It was damn interesting to think about those things all over again and it's like my mind was showing me some old invaluable snaps.

I am so confused about where my life was going.

Then, as my afternoon sessions were about to start I entered my classroom. Accordingly, classes started within few seconds. With each passing day Jack started avoiding me more and more. I was totally upset and I was like nothing. I did not know what I should do. All my friends were trying to divert my thought on something else as I was depressed and where everyone in my classroom, came down to me and asked; what happened to you? Why you are like this Deeksha?

It was a peaceful morning in the college campus, the next day. Once I sat at my desk in the classroom, I could see my close friends Meenu & Lalitha coming towards me. When they both reached my desk, Meenu and Lalitha asked; Deeksha shall we say something regarding Jack?. Though I kept quiet, they both started saying; Deeksha!! Jack was not a perfect match for you; we didn't say he's not good, but there are so many other persons in this world who are much better than him. We want one among those best person to be your hubby and not Jack. We know you will feel terrible when you hear both of our thoughts about Jack, but believe us that's the reality.

I did not know how to tell my friends that I couldn't even imagine a life without Jack because both my best friends always used to tell me the quote 'Thing's won't change unless we do'. Then, they both said, Deeksha cheer up, we want to see our old friend back and think twice about what we said regarding Jack. Also, they both added; Deeksha destiny is different from our wishes most of the times. I asked both my dear friends to give me some time to think over it. They agreed and said; take your own time Deeksha and then they left the place.

After giving a thought about my friend's words regarding Jack for a few weeks, I finally took a decision. I decided it's time to think about my friends alone. Also, I remembered Jack is one of my good friend apart from everything and Jack has known it very well too.

In addition, I felt making a million friends is not an achievement; but the real achievement is making one friend who stands by us through good and bad times. I remembered I had gotten a wonderful set of friends and I never want to miss my friends as well as their fun for any reason. Again, I remembered Jack was one among them.

But I can't help myself. Again, I thought; Jack somewhere inside of you, I exist. Somewhere between liking me, loving me and everything in the middle you get puzzled Jack. That prickly feeling horrifies you and you don't know in which direction to go. But this Deeksha knew she meant something to Jack even though Jack hides his real feelings. So I decided to find out the exact reason for Jack confusion. At the same time, I felt Jack can't run away from those feelings forever. On one day Jack was eventually going to accept the fact that I make his world go around. Also, I felt, I am lucky to have someone like Jack in my life.

But Jack had already stopped speaking to me and started avoiding me by the time. So, I did not want to get back with Jack. I decided it was time for me to move on. I understood, I needed to live for the present. But somewhere I still loved him and would get hurt when Jack would flirt with other girls from my batch in front of my very eyes.

It's already Christmas time heading before us, so the game called Chris Mom and Chris child started in all other gangs of our first year batch except our gang. It looked as if my friends had already planned it out and my name was also entered in the participants list. So before starting the game they invited me and once the game had started, everyone in the game picked up their Chris child's name which has been entered in a small paper. As everyone in the game had already chosen their Chris Child, all other contestants asked me to pick my Chris child's name. I was flabbergasted when I saw my Chris Child's name because I could see Jack name written in that paper.

Everyone in the game started asking who was it Deeksha? As each one was eager to know the name, though, as per game rules it should not be revealed out till the game gets over.

I grinned and went back to my desk without saying anything. Yes, it was so comical when the game started from next day onward. And conspicuously Jack was receiving more chocolates daily from her Chris Mom than all and sundry in the game. Plus, Jack was asked to do very little activities. It was really hilarious when each person in the game started doing one fun activity each day as per their Chris Mom order. Even I did not know who my Chris mom was. Each participant in game enthusiastically waited for our final finishing day of the game as we all wanted to know who our Chris Mom was's who asked us to do all those amusing activities. Also each one of us was excited about our unpredicted final day gifts.

In between the game Jack had a doubt regarding who his Chris Mom was, as he used to get more chocolates daily than all and sundry in the game. Jack thought it would be me. Thus, on one fine day, for all of a sudden Jack was asking irritably before everyone, could someone in game tell me who my Chris Mom was? Everyone laughed and said C'mon man; it was only a few more days left out of the game to get over. So play it right now Jack. Let's see who it was on the final finishing day of the game. Then Jack kept quiet. Yes, the game got over as days passed by. After a long wait, all and sundry, in the game got different gifts from their Chris Moms except Jack. But Jack didn't ask anything to anyone. And all my friends were busy with the gifts they received. Slowly, after few seconds I started walking towards Jack as he was sitting with a few of our friends at the last desk of classroom and chit chatting about all the gifts they received.

The minute, I reached the desk where Jack and few of our friends were sitting; these are for you Jack I said while handing him the gift I had brought to him. I was keeping my fingers crossed. Since I was not sure whether Jack would accept it or not. Immediately Jack said my presumption about my Chris Mom was precise.

Besides those words Jack accepted my gift and he opened it. I could hear a wow from everyone in the gang when Jack opened his gift as it was a wonderful flower vase made of glass with a yellow fluid filled in. Each one in the gang, including Jack knows yellow was this Deeksha's favorite color. But I didn't hear any comments from Jack about the gift yet. So, I was eagerly waiting to hear Jack comments. Yes, before I go, Jack said he didn't like that gift. I was down in the dumps after hearing those words. I felt Jack didn't like me at all and as I gave that gift to him; Jack said he didn't like it.

I walked back to my desk without saying anything and I started writing notes of my previous Physiology sessions held on that day. It's almost the last leisure hour of that day in college, so after finishing my notes I went back again to last desk where Jack and few of our friends were sitting and asked; Jack what gift do you want. After a small pause, I added; just let me know so that I could buy for you because you didn't like that gift right?. Jack said; I need a fish tank, a small one with two golden color fishes in it. I grinned and said; ok!!! By tomorrow you will get it.

We were around college closing hours of that day. Everybody was getting back to their desks to pack their college bags. Even I, Jack and few of our friends who all sat there at the last desk of classroom started moving back to our respective desks. As Jack desk was next to mine, he came behind me saying Deeksha it's too much. As I am your Chris child, you are going to give two gifts. Am I right? 'I know if it's someone else you won't do that' Jack said. Though I felt that was the fact, immediately I said 'No' you are wrong, nothing like that Jack.

After reaching our desks I started gathering my books which had been shattered on my desk and all my friends were also doing the same including Jack. Whoever had packed their college bags earlier said bye and left for the day.

Besides Jack came to my desk and handed over his Chris child gift, which I gave him, back to me. Jack said you take this gift back with you Deeksha, as I don't need it and please don't buy that fish tank gift which I had asked for.

I said ok, I won't buy anything more for you, but you have to take this gift back Jack because after all it was just a game. I kept the gift back on my desk and said; Jack even I won't take this gift back with me. Then I continued packing my college bag.

After a small pause, I again said; hope you understood Jack. Jack stood wordlessly near my desk for a few minutes, then Jack took the gift back with him and he left for the day without even saying bye to anyone of our friends including me.

In college, when I entered my classroom the next day, Jack came to me and said Deeksha thanks for such a wonderful gift. Though I was a little astounded, scandalized as well bemused at that minute, I remained hushed. Did you know I asked one of my hostel friends to keep some fresh flowers daily in that flower vase, Jack said. Then after a few seconds Jack added; I would take your gift to my hometown New Delhi and would keep it safe forever in my home. Without more ado, I asked Oh!! Really?!! Jack replied hey yes for sure. Hmm, good boy! I said with a wide smile on my face.

After that above conversation Jack again, never spoke to me. Jack started avoiding and irritating me utterly as like before. I felt it was time to think about my semester exams alone as our first year batch were nearing our first semester exams and we do have so many model papers left behind before leaving for Christmas holidays. Hence everybody started preparing for their exams.

I just wanted to show Jack that I didn't care for him anymore though I did it. Because I felt Jack himself will come back and speak with me soon. I thought for sure he would come back because Jack loves me.

I and all my friends, including Jack had much fun apart from our busy exam preparation schedules. We all were living in our own little world. A world of fun and enjoyment. I had never thought life in a medical college could be so much fun. Furthermore, I didn't think I would manage to get such wonderful friends.

Though Jack and I were together with our friends in college for the whole day looking at each other we both never spoke. Even Jack won't take lunch from my lunch box alone, even if our friends asked him to. Though I didn't say anything and kept quiet at those times; but that hurt me a bit because when Jack was speaking with me, he would be the first person to open my lunch box to taste my food.

In previous days when Jack and I were speaking with each other, Jack used to taste all our friends lunch only with my spoon. Though I used to say I licked the spoon, Jack would say; so what? Please Deeksha let me have lunch with this spoon itself.

Besides all those our batch was about to have our first semester model exams the next day morning.

In studies there had always been tough competition among our batch especially among our gang. Most probably the top mark holders of our batch (class first to class fifth/sixth) were from my gang.

I thought that my toughest competitors among my batch were my friends Divakar and Prakash especially.

I sat at my desk and started revising my lessons last time as there was only half an hour left for the model exams to get started.

I was looking into my notebook, but certain thoughts kept running in my mind that's I must be the topper of first year batch in the model as well as final exams and I should strive hard enough for it. Abruptly I could realize that someone was standing in front of my desk. So I took my gaze from my books to see who it was.

Yes, it was none other than Jack. Jack said, Hey Deeksha, I am really sorry. I was thunderstruck when Jack sat next to me because when Jack came to know that I love him, Jack was the one who moved to another row permanently, just because Jack doesn't want to sit behind my desk. But now Jack was sitting next to me. Jack asked how my exam preparations were going on. Though I became annoyed after hearing Jack words, I didn't want to concentrate on anything else until my first semester exams get over. Therefore, I replied hey Jack, yup; my exam preparations were going fine. So, how about yours? Hey its bit okay as I didn't go through all chapters wholly, Jack said.

In between our conversation, it looked like some of our friends who sat behind us started smiling and kidding both me and Jack, when they saw us together. We both didn't sense it as we were busy in talking about our exam preparations. And, only 15 minutes were left behind for our model exams to get started.

Suddenly one of our friends Sonia started shouting Jack! Jack! Once Jack and I turned back towards her, we both could see a big smile on Sonia's face. Immediately Sonia asked; Jack, why you were sitting there man?! And Prakash and Divakar started giggling and kidding Jack from their desks as Jack was sitting next to me. Sonia asked; Jack, what's special man? You are wearing yellow colour shirt today!! Then I and Jack realized that we both were wearing yellow colour dresses by coincidence and Jack said the same to Sonia.

After that, Sonia asked Jack to come to her desk. Swiftly we could see our first year in charge professor coming into our classroom with model exam question papers. So Jack sat with me again as the professor wanted to give a quick intro about exam timelines before distributing the question papers. And yes, Professor started shuffling our seats before our model exams. Jack had been shuffled to a different desk. Then exam started.

After finishing our model exam each one of us started discussing about our model exam papers. I was so happy and it was for 2 reasons. One was I wrote my model exam well. Second was Jack came and spoke back to me. So, I thought, yes, Jack loves me, that's why he came back. So it's time for us to leave for the day because we had one more model exam paper left out for the next day.

When, everyone started leaving for the day, I was packing my college bag yet. Once I heard Jack voice, I took my eyes from my college bag. And I could see Jack coming to my desk. Jack reached my desk and he said; hey Deeksha come we would leave together today and he asked where Sayina was?! As we 3 from our gang, used to leave for home together always.

I was unperturbed for a few seconds. Hey, once again, I am really sorry Deeksha, Jack said. Please forget everything. Above all I am one of your closest friends Deeksha and we won't get back these college days. It's only this 4 and half years, after that life would be different for each one of us. Really, I felt somewhat bad after I fought with you;

Immediately I interrupted and said; I never felt anything like that Jack. Then Jack asked; oh!! Is it? Hey! Then is it only me who feels in such a way?! I kept quiet again. Jack one more time, said; come we will leave together Deeksha. Finally, after so much of the argument we both left together as Sayina had left with our classmate Devaki.

Yes, again, I could see the same old Jack who was so close to me. We started chatting regularly through messages. We started speaking with each other daily. Sometimes Jack said; hey Deeksha, you recharge my mobile number for this month as I had more expenses this month and I would recharge your mobile number next month so that we could continue speaking like this for more than hours and the call ends up like hey Deeksha, I don't know how far I came from my room as I started walking away slowly from my room, after receiving your call. I used to say; oh ok, then get back to the room and just drop me a message, bye will see you tomorrow Jack.

Likewise, on one day, Jack started speaking about his Mom, how she doesn't want him to leave college hostel and vacate to a new house with his friends because she used to say Jack would spoil himself if he stay outside of college hostel and how Jack was totally frustrated about it.

After hearing all those, I slowly started thinking about Jack personal diary and how he felt regarding his Mom and Uncle's words regarding an incident in school days and also the challenge he had undertaken to prove them that he won't be bad and for sure he would not speak anything despite the consequences before he gets a job and earns money on his own.

I was flabbergasted when I heard one more incident from Jack. On one weekend when he was there in the hostel, all our class guys, including Jack went to our classmate Tineesh room merely. Suddenly some of our class boys said why we should not watch a porn movie, and then everyone over there agreed to it. Jack said; Deeksha but I left in-between to the hostel. Deeksha that was the biggest mistake I had done in life and I promise you I won't do it anymore in my life. Believe me, that was the first time, I watched a porn movie and that too because of a few of our class guys compulsion. Once again, Jack mentioned, I am really sorry for doing that Deeksha and I won't do it any more in my life. I was stunned as well as irritated to hear all those but I kept quiet while hearing it from Jack. As well, certain thoughts started running in my mind, why Jack should say all these to me, does he love me?!

When I came back to my senses, I could hear Jack piercing voice; hey Deek's are you there? Hey, sorry Jack, yes, I am here, I said. Jack said; I know you are thinking very badly about me and you don't want to be my friend right? I interrupted and said hey C'mon Jack I didn't say anything like that. Anyways, leave that topic and speak about something else Jack. At last the call ended in the usual way.

Once I ended Jack call on that day and after retiring to bed that night I thought lots about his awfully sorry. I was thinking again and again does Jack love me? It seems yes, but after he read my love for him on my personal diary on that day, why did Jack say he doesn't have any feelings like that for me as well a Sorry for if he had behaved to me in such a way.

I again and again thought about it and I felt Jacks loves me for sure, but he hides it from me for some reason. So I thought to find out the exact reason before the 4 and half years (my college days) ends out.

Yes, the next day in college, another model exam paper was over and our whole first year batch left home earlier. And we had one more working day before Christmas holidays, just to give out our model exam marks. Yes, the next day everyone was very eager to know who got class first in our model exams. I was really excited to know who got first. I said to myself; would it be Divakar, Prakash or me? And finally, yes, it was me who scored 98 percentages being the class topper and Prakash got class second with 95 percentages while Divakar occupied 6th place.

I was ecstatic. Though all my friends were glad for me, they all were still a bit dreary as they didn't make it to the class top. After issuing our marks Professor asked the class toppers to come front and Professor asked the rest of the class to give a big round of applause for both of us. The professor said; Deeksha keep up your good marks and do well in final exams as well.

Besides, the professor said congrats to Prakash too, and asked him what made him to score 95 and not 98. Prakash explained the reason for it. Prakash had one more chapter, which was yet to be covered by him and he would be covering that chapter before his final exams. The professor asked; Prakash will you defeat Deeksha's marks in the final exam and vice versa. When we both said we would score 100 percentages in the finals. The professor said, let's see who's getting top marks in first year batch and he said, congrats once again to both Prakash and me. Professor congratulated everyone in class for our good percentages overall as well wished everyone to do well in the final exams. The professor conveyed his advance Christmas and New Year wishes to everyone. Anyways, happy holidays, let's meet in the New Year, the professor added and then he left for the department staff room.

In our first year batch 90 percent of students were hostilities and only 10 percent are localities of Bangalore. So, host élites started leaving swiftly for the day as they want to get back to their hometowns because after joining college it was our first long holidays we got that too after a long struggle with college management. Though I felt a bit sad to leave all my friends, especially Jack, but at the same time I was happy to meet all my family members after a long back as I was never away from home till my schoolings and I remembered how my Mom cried one whole day when I came to the hostel. Thus, I said bye to almost all my friends and a few classmates of mine. Yet I had to say bye only to my friends Kiran and Jack. When I met Kiran to say bye, he said; wait! I will take you to Jack; you ask him whatever you want from Delhi, as it seems each one had asked Jack to buy certain things from his home town. Kiran wontedly took me to Jack, while Jack stood near the entrance of our first year classroom and he was wishing happy journey to one of our classmates.

In front of Jack, Kiran said; Deeksha now ask Jack whatever you want from New Delhi and Kiran was waiting there to see both our rejoinder. Then, Jack asked me in a sluggish tone, hey Deeksha tell me what you want from my hometown and before I opened my mouth to ask, Kiran said; hey Deeksha ask him to bring some sweets. I said; no, I don't want anything Jack. You just go home safely and come back safely to Bangalore that's enough for me. Jack asked in a bit louder tone, what?!! Come again!! And I repeated the same one more time to Jack. In between we both could see Kiran smiling at both of us. Then Kiran went inside the classroom to pack his college bag as he had not done yet. Jack anyhow, my hearty advance wishes for a merry Christmas and Happy New Year and happy journey as well I said and I waved bye. Jack in return replied Thanks Deeksha!! Happy journey!! Take care, bye. I smiled at Jack and left the place.

As my Trichy trip with Sonia, Shamili and their hostel friends had been cancelled; I went to my hometown for Christmas holidays. Yes, its again pleasurable days for everyone at our home with our families. I felt, I was missing all my friends, especially Jack. Even some of my friends felt the same, so they called me through phone and spoke with me for a few minutes. Likewise, on one day when my friend Sonia called me; she said it seems every one of our friends was missing everyone and she added who had called her through the phone in the past week. And the list had Jack name.

The moment Sonia ended her call; I was thinking why Jack didn't call me. I became irate. Also, I felt, why I should not call Jack? Then certain issues struck my mind that's Jack mobile would be in roaming. But I could call to his home. Again, what would happen if someone else picks the call what would I say? Because Jack, Mom was so strict. And might be that's how Jack doesn't have more close friends from school days. Then I murmured to myself, let me see what happens!! Let me call to Jack home number.

I tried calling Jack from my mobile number. Yes, someone picked my call and to my bombshell it was none other than Jack. I said, Hi Jack, how are you? How was everyone at home? Jack replied hey

Deeksha what a surprise! I am good and everyone here is good too. Hope you are fine too. Then Jack asked how everyone was at my home? How about our friends? Did anyone call you? I remained silent for a few seconds, and then I asked why didn't you call me Jack? You spoke with our friend Sonia it seems.Jack said, I am really sorry Deeksha. Please forgive your Jack okay. Come again, Jack!! I said. Jack replied, I meant couldn't you forgive your friend Jack for not calling you. I laughed and asked Oh is it?!!

In the meanwhile I could hear some background voice and it looked as if Jack, Mom was speaking to someone over there. May be their neighbor/guest, whoever had come to their home. But Jack spoke continuously as well slowly with me for a few more minutes where his Mom could not hear it. Jack again said; Deek's don't mistake me for not calling you. Anyways, let's see in college in another few days Deeksha and bye for now Jack said and he hung up.

It was the end of our vacations. Going back to college was not an exciting thought at all but being with wonderful friends makes us to. The world would definitely be a better place with more people like them. I still remember the first day we all met. We all were too shy to talk then and look at us now! We have become the best of friends.

Yes, college reopened after Christmas holidays on Jan 3rd 2006.But, the classroom was not yet opened as the housekeeping in charge said our classroom keys were missing and he went ahead to check with Dental department. Also, he asked every one of us to wait near our classrooms itself. One more advantage of that beautiful college campus was we had the whole view of college campus almost from each building. So, we could see everyone standing outside the classroom when we were a bit far away from our department. So, when I was on my way to the classroom, I could see all my friends standing together except Jack and Sonia as they both were chit chatting with our north Indian classmates.

I reached my gang and said Hi all. All my friends started kidding me, instantly. Hey Deeksha did you see Jack, he had already come.

I smiled and said, hey C'mon, I saw him already and he was there chit chatting with our north Indian gang.

Meanwhile we could see housekeeping in charge opening the classroom lock and once the door was opened everyone started entering the classroom. Then there was a strident din inside the classroom as each one was speaking with their friends about what they did on vacation. And even Jack was speaking to all our friends, but Jack never spoke with me yet. Whenever I saw him, he turned towards some other side and pretended like he didn't see me at all.

I felt something was wrong. In between, we all could see our Physiology professor entering our classroom and the class had a pin drop silence then. Our 1st lecture of 2nd semester had gone almost for more than one hour. The subjects were not as easy as the ones we had in 1st semester. It was a bit tricky. Then, we had a leisurely hour. I could see Jack speaking with Meenu with his mobile in hand and it seemed Jack had changed his mobile number. Hence he was giving missed calls to Meenu so that she could save his number in her mobile.

I went ahead and spoke with Jack; but I could see Jack getting back to his respective desk swiftly without any response. I felt so bad; I went back and sat in the last desk of my classroom with my Physiology notes. My friends Meenu, Lalitha and I all three of us always used to sit together to study in our leisure hours. Lalitha and Meenu slowly came to the last desk of the classroom with their books. Meenu and Lalitha said; Deeksha, you know about Jack right, Jack himself would come and speak with you after some time or some days, so don't worry. Even after hearing those words I felt dreadful, but nodded my head to my friends.

At the end of that day Jack didn't say bye to me, but he waved bye to all my friends and then Jack left along with Divakar and Prakash. After going home, I was about to call Jack by 8:00pm as I got his new mobile number from my friend Meenu. When Jack received my call he asked who's that and then how did you get my number. I in turn asked; Jack I have only one question for you? Why didn't you talk to me today? Please answer my question. I will end the call and I won't call you anymore.

I was just shaken when Jack yelled at me. Why did you call to my home on that day? And because you asked me, I said sorry continuously for not calling you and it seemed my Mom heard everything I spoke to you. After ending your call on that day did you know how much scolding's did I get? From mom. Deeksha, I can tell you one thing for sure now. You should never call to my home anymore from now onward. After a small pause, Jack said, but you can call to my mobile number anytime. I felt execrable after hearing it. Thus, I said don't worry Jack I won't call you anymore, not even to your mobile number. Jack again said; I never told you not to call to my mobile number. I said bye and ended the call immediately.

I kept thinking to myself; why is it always me? But I knew it was my mistake. It was all because I had taken the worst decision of life by being loving this person. I felt everything was over about my love and my heart felt so heavy. Lying on the bed, thoughts started flowing in my head along with tears on my face. I could also see my lips murmuring continuously, No God! It should not be that way!! Jack should come back and speak with me again as usual.

The next day morning in college I could see Jack coming to my desk after our classes got over while I was busy in copying my Physiology running notes into fair copy. Jack came near me and said hey Deeksha just move a little and sit as I was sitting in the middle of the desk where no one else can sit in that desk. Jack said; he wanted to sit next to me. I stared at him; Jack said hey C'mon move and sit I want to speak with you for a few minutes. Jack, I don't want to speak with you, so you better move out from here, I said. Jack smiled and said; Deeksha move or else I will sit on your lap and when Jack pretended like he was about to sit on my lap, I moved immediately to the other end of the desk. Jack laughed and said, oh God finally I got seated next to Deeksha, so now I think I could speak with my friend Deeksha. I didn't react to his words and kept copying my notes.

Jack asked me to listen to him for a few minutes and he started telling me, hey my Mom scolded me very badly on that day after your phone call Deeksha and that made me feel stumpy. And I am really sorry Deeksha. I dumped all those anger and depression within myself from that day and showed off all my anger on you yesterday. We could show our anger only on our close ones Deeksha. As you are my close friend I showed off all my anger on you Deeksha. It's nothing like you should not speak with me, but don't ever call my home Deeksha, as I think you know about my Mom very well. But you can call me at any time to my mobile number. Hope you understand my situation and now it's your wish to speak with me or not. Jack added; I don't want to lose my Friend for any reason. Anyhow, you continue copying notes and he went back to his respective desk.

The same day afternoon Jack came to my desk and took my lunch box to taste my food. Immediately I screamed, hey Jack stop!! Jack kept the spoon back in the lunch box along with food and asked what? I said; you take someone else spoon either Meenu's or someone else Jack because I licked my spoon completely as I had food with ghee as it's my favorite, that's why asked you to stop.

Jack said, oh that's it and he had food with the same spoon, then, while all our friends laughed at Jack. After that, he said okay, it's enough, let me go to the hostel and have my hostel food also a bit and come back. Then Jack left the classroom.

I started having my lunch thinking Jack was always different and he gives no clue of what he was thinking in his heart about others and especially about me. Why this guy always picks only my spoon to taste food either it's fresh or used by me. I again murmured 'No way it's really difficult to understand him'. Suddenly I could hear my friend's voice loudly. Hey Deeksha have your food soon, at least today, so that we could go for a walk and to canteen to buy your favorite Diary milk chocolates. Hurry up or else we will leave you and go, they said. Hey, no! Wait! I will have my food soon so that I could join you guys. After lunch I had a nice time with my friends with so much fun.

On the same day once I reached my room after college, my father called me and said he was near to Bangalore; he came for some other work, and as he came that much near to Bangalore, he thought to come and see me once. My father added, he would leave Bangalore by next day morning. I said; okay dad!! I had already reached my room. Once my father reached Bangalore, we both went to my cousin's house.

All of a sudden I could see Jack name flashing on my mobile screen. After picking Jack call, I said; Hey Jack I am in my sister home as my father had come down. So I would call you back,after getting back to my room might be after 9.00pm.Jack interrupted and said; hey listen to me Deeksha, shall I come and meet your father now?. I was astounded and asked why you want to meet him now?! Jack said; simply, I just wish to see him. Anyways, I will be there in another 5 minutes. I think your sister home was very nearby from my room like yours but anyway you just tell me the way once Deeksha.

I couldn't stop Jack from coming to my cousin's house as he didn't listen to my words. Jack said, he wanted to meet my dad that day. Above all I was amazed as well, dazed, and at the same time I don't know what Jack was going to speak with my father. Ultimately, I flocked my mettle and told my dad and cousin that one of my close friends named Jack was coming home just to meet dad in another 5 minutes.

In between I could see Jack name blinking on my mobile screen again. As soon as I picked his call, Jack told he was waiting in front of my sister building and he asked shall I come upstairs?! Yup, sure Jack, I said. After that, Jack and my dad started speaking and whenever I interrupted in between Jack said you keep quiet Deeksha. I am asking about you from your dad and not from you. Jack was continuously asking the entire details about me from my dad and in between my dad said; Jack, I have seen you guys (Deeksha, Jack and all your friends) talking and chatting for long times at night. Dad added; it's better to sleep early and to get up early in the morning. It would be good for health and for your studies too. Finally, after an hour after getting so much info about me from my dad, Jack said; okay, Uncle I simply came to meet you as I came this way for a shop. My dad said that's okay, Jack. Jack in turn said, ok, I will leave now as its already late, bye for now and will see you sometime later uncle. Okay!! Deeksha let's meet in college tomorrow, bye, Jack said and he left.

After reaching my room, I tried to Jack mobile number thrice, leaving a 10 minute gap in between each call but Jack didn't pick up the call. I tried to Meenu number and asked her to bring her Physiology book as Meenu had some different author and I asked Meenu; did Jack contacted you today evening? Meenu said; yes, he called me just a few minutes back and he too asked for physiology book. Oh is it? I just called him thrice. He didn't pick my call and that's why asked you? Meenu. Anyways, let's meet in college tomorrow. Bye Meenu I said and I hung up. I was thinking what happened to this Jack!! Just now Jack himself came down to meet my dad and now he was not even picking my calls. I felt, I can ask about that in college the next day to Jack .Hence, I slept off.

Next day, it's as usual morning first hour in college where everyone was busy with their yesterday physiology notes as there will be a petite quiz daily from yesterdays portion from our Physiology professor before she starts her class and whoever doesn't answer even for a single question out of 3 that person should listen that day class by standing outside the classroom.

Within few seconds we all could see our Physiology professor entering our classroom. The classes got over almost after an hour or more and the next hour was a leisure hour for our batch. Hence, before I started asking for the book, Meenu came to my desk and gave me her Physiology book which I asked her yesterday. Also Meenu said; Jack didn't pick your calls as he doesn't want to bother you.

When Jack met your dad yesterday, it seems he asked Jack to stop calling, or chatting with you at nights as it would be good for your studies and health. Jack said it looked like your wish and you just asked your dad to convey it to Jack. Hence Jack doesn't want to disturb you as per your wish and that's why he didn't pick your calls yesterday.

Additionally, Jack said he won't call you or talk to you anymore Deeksha as he doesn't want to disturb you anymore. Oh!! Is it?!! Meenu. I never said anything to my dad and he didn't say it to Jack alone, he said commonly if we sleep earlier on our college days it would be easy to get up early in the morning, that's what my father had mentioned and it's my dad's opinion alone that's it. But Jack had understood it in different way it seems Meenu. Anyways, just give me some time I will give you a letter Meenu. Can you just give it to Jack please?! I said; once I finish writing a letter, I will come to your desk Meenu, I added. Hence Meenu went back to her desk.

As I don't want to speak with Jack anymore, I wrote a letter. The content of that letter was; I felt there was always misunderstandings and unnecessary fights between both of us. So I decided to keep an end to Jack friendship as it would be easier for me to concentrate on my studies.

On the other hand, I came to this wonderful university just to study and for nothing else. I started explaining the fact about what my dad said in that letter. I added; I won't expect Jack to talk with me anymore as because my Friend Jack was dead a day before. If he would have been alive he would have understood about me as well if something went wrong in between both of us, Jack would have asked me straight away. Jack won't convey it through any of our friends.

Also, I am sorry for my dad's words Jack, regardless of whether it's good or not. I won't come and ask you to speak with me anymore as you are not my friend and it's your wish as I am just your classmate. Then, I walked to Meenu desk and gave her the letter and asked her to just give it to Jack.

Next, I asked my friends Meenu and Lalitha to come with Physiology books to the last desk in the classroom where we three used to study together or take notes together from books of different authors. Once we three assembled together at the last desk in the classroom, we started to take notes and also started thinking about our first year final exams.

Lalitha said; we have to study well and secure excellent scores this year as it would help us to prove ourselves among our batch, while Meenu and I were nodding our heads and in between those we could see Jack coming towards our last desk. Jack came and stood in front of me as I was sitting in the middle of the desk whereas Meenu was sitting next to me on one side and Lalitha vice versa. Jack asked hesitatingly, hey Deeksha!! You won't speak to me? Though I saw him, I remained unperturbed while Meenu and Lalitha were taking notes continuously.

Jack added; Deeksha, you told your friend Jack had died. So, tell me as per which religion you want to do my funerals. Hindu?! Or Christian?! I was shaken and I gaped at Jack face for a while. But Jack was recurrently asking me the same. Deeksha! As per which religion you want my funeral to take place? Tell me, please!

I was thinking why this Jack was asking like this? Does he love me? Otherwise, why he has to ask whether his funeral has to be done as per my Hindu religion? Then, my mind words started echoing; Hey Jack! I know you love me and you want everything even your funeral to happen according to my wish. But you never knew, Deeksha don't want to live without Jack and my wish would always be to leave this wonderful journey of life before you Jack. So it's always your wish to do Deeksha's funeral in whichever way you want Jack, as I am and I will always be yours.

Jack started speaking stridently waving his hand before my eyes. Hey Deeksha are you here in this world?!! Then, I came back to my senses, stopped gawking at Jack and I glanced at my books. In between all this, Lalitha and Meenu said; Deeksha just call us, once you guys finish off speaking about this and they left back to their respective desks. Jack came and sat next to me and when he saw me looking at my books, Jack said; hey Deeksha look at me and answer my question. I saw my friend's desk as they all were having so much fun, altogether. I felt I wanted to be there with my friends. I could also see my whole batch having so much of fun, except a very few who were walking here and there in the classroom. Besides, I could hear Jack loud voice again. I am sorry Deeksha and I won't do it anymore.

I kept quiet for a few more minutes. I didn't eavesdrop to Jack words. I felt, life could be much better if we search for love and run behind true friends. Afterwards, I left the place. As it's only a few minutes left out for my anatomy sessions to begin. I wished to join my gang, as they all were having so much fun over there. I joined my gang, had so much of fun for a few minutes. Then we could see all other students of our class started leaving to anatomy labs at its time, so our gang too started.

Once the classes were over for that day, everyone started leaving for home and as Sayina was on leave, I thought, oh today I have to leave alone till front gate!! So I packed my college bags and left quickly.

The moment I came down to ground floor I could hear someone's voice, which said Hey Deeksha! Wait, I would join you and when I turned to see who it was, it was none other than Jack. So, I didn't stop for him, but Jack came running and joined me.

Jack again started saying, hey Deeksha! I am really sorry, yaar. Please speak to me. I kept on walking without saying anything to Jack. In between Jack met one of his hostel friends on the way and he was none other than Sonashk from BDS first year batch. Thus Jack stopped there.

Subsequently, I walked fast, so that Jack won't join me, but to my surprise, I could see Jack coming in bike with his hostel friend. His friend left Jack near me said bye and went. Again, Jack said; hey Deeksha wait, I am not able to walk that fast like you.

At length I stopped on my way and said; hey Jack! C'mon, leave for hostel yaar. Ok!! I will leave if you accept me as your friend and agree to have a juice with me, Jack said! At long last after so much of arguments, I said; ok, but before that I don't want my friend Jack to ask sorry to me anymore.

On the contrary, this Deeksha can understand you and your thoughts, but my problem was why Jack didn't come and ask me straight away if there was any problem with me. Why did Jack convey it through someone else and he had never done like that before, though he had a few misunderstandings with me earlier? Those times Jack just came and asked me right away. And I liked that attitude of yours, Jack, and that's my friend.

But now! That's why I felt my friend Jack was no more. Anyhow, I am sorry Jack and don't speak like that anymore i.e., asking about your funerals and all. I really felt terrible. Deeksha then why did you write like that in your letter that I am dead, Jack asked. I did it because you made me too. I said. Okay, let us forget about it and will be good friends like before, Jack said.

Anyways, come, let us have some Juice, I said. Yup, sure!! But you have to pay the bill, as I didn't bring my purse, Jack said. I just smiled and said okay. Jack added; but no fruit juices try Maaza today. What!! I never like it, Jack. It's good; you just try it at least for the sake of my words Deeksha.

At last Jack made me to drink half liter Maaza and when I was about to pay the bill Jack took his purse and paid the bill. I was surprised and hushed for a few seconds. Then Jack saw me, grinned and said come let's leave. Yup!! But before that; I need those Cadbury chocolates, Jack. We would come some other time again; Deeksha. I would buy and give you your favorite Cadbury chocolates that time. Ok Jack!! I said with a grin on my face. But I murmured to myself; oh you would come with me alone like this again Jack!! Ok, bye Deeksha, Jack said. I liked Maaza, Jack! Ok bye; go safely. See you tomorrow in college Jack said with a wide smile on his face.

The next day morning once I reached my classroom, I just kept my college bag on my desk. I could hear Meenu voice saying hey

Deeksha what it seems someone had come in bike to catch you yesterday, are you walking that fast Deeksha? I smirked at Meenu and asked who told you all that.

Meenu smiled and said I heard through someone. I could also see a few of my friends who had arrived a bit early were smiling at me after hearing Meenu words. Slowly, after a few minutes every one of our classmates arrived including Jack. Also, we all could see our Physiology professor entering our classroom.

Once our Physiology classes were over for the day, I, Meenu and Lalitha sat at the last desk in the classroom where we usually gather together to take notes. Meenu again started kidding me and gradually I told that we went to Juice shop which was next to our college front gate and I said I like Maaza now. As me, Meenu and Lalitha were the closest friends among our gang there won't be any secrets between us. I, Meenu and Lalitha always use to share all our life happenings with each other.

After taking notes, we three went back to our respective desks. We had 15 more minutes left out for our next session. Hence Jack came to Meenu desk simply to chit chat for a few seconds. Once Jack reached Meenu desk, she smiled at Jack and asked; what Jack I heard Maaza was good yesterday? Was it? Jack looked amazing after hearing it and Jack stared at me from there.

I pretended like I didn't hear anything and didn't see Jack at all. As Jack was wordless, he went back to his desk swiftly. When Jack and I were leaving for home on that day, Jack asked me why you said everything to Meenu and Lalitha. Won't you be able to maintain certain secrets? Nothing like that Jack!! They both were my close friends and we don't have any secrets in between us. So, I told them. Oh is it?!! Ok! Then go and tell them this also. About what you speak with me today, Jack said. After that, I kept quiet.

In college, the next day Meenu started kidding Jack with that Maaza story again. Jack became angry and said; Meenu I will buy and give Maaza to you all. But never ever kid either me or Deeksha with this maaza story anymore. Ok!! But first you buy and give us Maaza, and then I won't do it for sure Jack, Meenu said. Ok, today evening after college, we will go to canteen. I will give you all a treat, Jack said. After college, I said to all my friends, ok!! You guys enjoy, I will leave for the day.

Instantaneously Jack said; hey Deeksha but before you leave I need to speak with you for 5 minutes. So just wait. I asked what?!! Then Jack turned towards all our friends and they said ok!! You speak with Deeksha and come quickly. We will wait for you in canteen Jack. Once they left, Jack came near me and asked, hey Deeksha if I discontinue my course and go back to my hometown New Delhi what you will think about me? I was bemused after hearing Jack words and asked what?!! Please come again, Jack!! Deeksha, you reply me first, Jack said.

After a small pause, I said; I would think I have lost a good friend, but Jack you tell me why you are asking like this? No!! My mother was asking me to come back and join some other course in New Delhi itself because this is too far known, so I might be discontinuing but I am not sure as of now, Jack said. After hearing it, I was taken aback!! Jack again asked; so, Deeksha, you will think you had lost a good friend that's it? Yes!! Why? Jack, I said. Hey, no!! Nothing!! You leave for the day Deeksha, I have to go and join our friends, and they would be waiting there in canteen for me. Bye, Jack Sighed and left for the canteen.

When I started walking alone, I was thinking why Jack asked me like that. I never knew what Jack expected me to say? But I don't want him to go back to his hometown. I felt; Jack was more than a friend to me and even Jack knows that very well. Nevertheless, you don't leave from here and I hope you won't because you love me Jack.

As days went on slowly we were nearing our first semester final exams. The college management started checking our fee paid structures. Finally, our batch got study holidays for around 2 weeks. We all were asked to come and collect our hall tickets three days before our semester exams.

Everyone in our batch started saying we all will miss our days of togetherness and fun for 15 more days, but it's time to prove our talents on subject knowledge. So, focus on our subjects alone. Then, we started leaving for the day saying hey all the best guys; see you all on the day of the exam.

I strived hard from the next day. My wish was to get university top and get a merit medal before whole students of that university. Also, I want the whole university to feel proud of my department. I know it's not easy because I didn't wish for a class or department topper but university topper. I remember thinking to myself nothing is impossible in this world. Also, I felt I had to prove everyone, even a girl from a small town could prevail all Bangalore school students as well as North Indian CBSE Students Knowledge wise. I realized that's not a big deal until I have very strong subject knowledge.

I remembered Jack words being a topper of model exams. Jack said; Deeksha let's see in final exams. If Jack himself is ready for a challenge!! Then, why Deeksha should not? I said by the time. Jack angrily said. Do you remember that I am a CBSE student?. I asked; so what?!! Jack. Deeksha remember you are a state board student, so whatever subjects you guys studied in 10th STD the CBSE students had gone through it in 8thSTD itself.

I smirked at him and asked so what?!! Anyways, Okay!! I accept your challenge Jack. I would be the topper this time in final exams, I said by the time. Jack said, let's see and left the place. So, my contemplation was I have to reach university top for sure in my first semester exams. And it's only one more day left behind for my final exams. Hence, I started revising my subjects for the final time.

On the day of the exam, everyone arrived an hour before the exam time to college. I reached just half an hour before the examination time, all my classmates, including my friends were still cramming up. Almost everyone used to read until the very end, but I could not find Prakash anywhere. Might be he's not arrived yet.

From a distance I just waved my hands to all my friends. Then I went and sat at the last desk of third row as all other desk was occupied by all my classmates and their shattered notes. As I don't want to revise anything as it's only half an hour left out for exams, I started arranging all my pens in my pouch which I could carry to my exam hall. By the time I could see Jack coming to my desk.

Jack came and sat next to me. Jack said Oye topper and teased me. I said shut up yaar. Jack again teased me and asked; Deeksha so finally are you done with the exam preparations? I smirked and didn't say anything. So, done with your exam preparations? Jack!! I asked.

Yup!! I had gone through the concepts of all chapters. I think I can make it, but I need a small help from you as well Deeksha. I didn't understand a chapter from Sociology. Can you just give a brief explanation of that chapter Deeksha!! So that it would be more helpful for me to make it in exam if it's asked for.

When I was about to explain that chapter to Jack I could see Prakash entering the classroom. He went and sat along with Divakar. Then Prakash started searching for Jack.

At last, when Prakash saw Jack next to me, Prakash had a big smile on his face and said; Divakar!! Even I searched where Jack was; he was sitting in the right place only!! Though I sat at a distance, I could hear Prakash words, but I pretended like I didn't hear anything.

Simultaneously on the other side, I could hear Jack loud tone; hey Deeksha please explain me that chapter soon as its already getting late and its only few more minutes left out. We have to reach our exam halls at least 15 minutes earlier. In between all those I could also hear Meenu tone asking me to explain about same chapter. Hence Jack said; Meenu even I, am asking her to explain me the same chapter.

At last, I started explaining them that chapter very shortly as we had less time. Meanwhile, we all could hear from one of our professors that everyone has to go to their respective exam halls without delay, as it's only 10 minutes left off for the exams to start. And the professor stood at the entrance of our first year classroom and again asked everyone to move immediately to our exam halls.

I always felt my best competitor in my class was my friend Prakash. So I decided the topper of that first year batch should either be Prakash or I. In case if we both were not able to make it to top, then it should be someone from my gang.

When I turned towards Prakash, I could see Prakash pulling his pens and sketches in a hurry from his bag. I went near Prakash and said; Hey hi Prakash!! Have you done with your exam preparations? Prakash in turn asked; what you were going to do with my preparations Deeksha and why you want to know it. I felt dreadful after hearing that. Anyways, all the best Prakash, I said. Prakash with a big smile on his face said All the best to you too Deeksha!

Then I left my classroom and reached the exam hall. Everything looked new for everyone, the big university exam hall, the different batch students and the seating arrangements with one senior in between each one of us. I checked out which bench I had. Finally, we all were sitting on our respective benches and waiting for our professors to enter the exam hall. Our professors entered the exam hall and they handed over the question papers. I was going over the question paper. I attempted for full marks.

After finishing our exams we all left our exam halls, one by one slowly. I could see Jack, Kiran, Sonia and a few of my other friends and classmates were waiting outside the exam hall while some others left and some were leaving by the time. Deeksha 100 out of 100 right? Kiran asked. Anticipating in the vicinity of 97.Let's see because we have one more exam right? I said with a wide grin on my face. Hey Deeksha come, let's leave for the day. It's already late. Jack said. Jack Where is Sayina? It seems she already left with our classmate Devaki. Come, let's go, Jack said.

Hey wait, I will also join you people as I have to go to the bus stop which was on the way to Deeksha room, Kiran said. As soon as we 3 were near to the boy's hostel which was inside the college premises Jack said bye to us and he left for the hostel. And when Kiran reached the bus stop, he said ok Deeksha go safely, bye, see you tomorrow.

Again, after half a day revisions everyone was present at the exam hall the next day morning. The second paper was also easy. We all were satisfied with our performances based on whatever we studied. After exams, the whole Physiotherapy department was excited to know about semester holidays. We got a month vacation, everyone was happy and started screaming in joy exception was Bangalore students. We all could hear happy holiday wishes from all the sides. Then one by one started leaving for the day, at a snail's pace.

In my gang except Jack, Divakar, Shamili, Sonia and me all others were from Bangalore. Hence, they all said; ok guy's happy journey and convey our wishes to all your families and please buy something for us from your hometowns. At last, almost most of them left for the day.

Enthusiastically I could hear Shamili and Sonia voice. Hey Deeksha, you come to the college hostel with us and we will have lunch in college hostel. We 3 can go to your room then, so that you can take your luggages and from there we will go together till Bangalore Bus Terminal and from there we can depart.

My friends Prakash, Kiran, Somesh from my gang too wished 3 of us happy journeys and when they were about to leave, Divakar said; he would join them, as he was leaving Bangalore by evening. What about you Jack when was your train, Divakar asked. It's today evening 5 pm, me and our classmate Shanwar will be leaving together till railway station and from there we would depart, Jack said. Hence Divakar asked Jack to join them. Then except Jack, all others started walking slowly towards the bike shed.

Suddenly I turned back, when I heard Jack tone. Deeksha, you are leaving now, right? Yes!! Let's see after a month. Bye for now. I have to go to the girl's hostel in another 5 minutes otherwise Sonia and Shamili would kill me. I have to leave now. So Bye, Happy Journey and convey my wishes to your family members, Take care. See you after a month Jack, I said and then I started walking towards the girls' hostel.

Again, I could hear Jack tone. Hey, Deeksha! I turned back and asked what!! Jack kept quiet. Hey, C'mon, leave along with Divakar, go join them Jack. See there. They all were near to the bike shed, I said. Okay!! Happy Journey, Bye, Jack said. Afterwards, Jack started walking towards the bike shed, gradually.

Next, it was splendid hours for me with my friends Sonia and Shamili where we had so much fun and it was really a nice journey to our hometowns. After reaching home, I was so happy to share with my Parents about my first university exams. By the time, I could hear my mind voice; yes, I am going to make it to university top this time. But I didn't say anything about it to my parents. Anyways, I had awesome days with my family members.

Chapter 2

It was the end of our first semester vacations and beginning of 2nd semester. Everyone in my batch of Physiotherapy department had come again from hometowns on the college reopening day exception was north Indians. We all were cheery to see everybody after the one month period of time. Just thinking about our fun times altogether brought dimples back on most of our faces.

As it was the first day of 2nd semester, classes were not commenced yet. We had much of the fun altogether. It was just a pleasant afternoon where my whole gang sat altogether and started chit chatting and having so much of fun. Suddenly someone from my gang said hey guys listen, someone mobile was ringing, so check your mobiles please. Yes, it was none other than Meenu's.

Once Meenu picked the call, she asked all our friends to be quiet for a few minutes. Then Meenu started speaking loudly, hey Jack how you are? And when you were coming back to Bangalore? It was almost an hour Jack was speaking to all our friend's except to Deepika and me.

Meenu asked one of our friends to hand over the mobile to me. Then she asked me to speak with Jack. No! No!! I don't want to speak, I said. Somehow, finally I could hear a hello from Jack. Hey!! How you are and how is everyone at home Jack? I am fine Deeksha. Then there was a long silence on both ends. So how is everyone at home? I asked, again. The moment I asked him, I could hear Jack's shrill voice on the other end, which said; Deeksha, you just want to speak with me only to ask this? Yes, Jack, I said. Instantaneously Jack asked me to hand over the mobile to Deepu. What!! I asked. Please give the mobile to Deepu; Jack again said stridently as well, harshly and so I did. Then I remember thinking to myself; I didn't know what Jack wants me to speak?

The instant Deepu ended Jack's call. I told my friends; Hey guys just listen to me for a few seconds. When I asked about his family to Jack; he just reacted to me in such a way!! Hey Deeksha, you just want to speak with me only to ask this? Jack said!! Why did Jack say like that? I asked all my friends.

After a small pause, yes!! Why did Jack ask like that only to you? My whole gang altogether said in a curious voice. And within microseconds all my friends broke into laughter. Hey, C'mon , it's nothing special, I hollered. Simply he would have asked me like that, I said. Oh is it?!! All my friends shouted!! Yes!! Might be!! I said.

Then, almost a week was over and not even a single north Indian student has come back from their vacations yet. We got an announcement from the college management that our 2nd semester classes would get continued from next week onwards.

 Next week, it was just an exquisite Monday morning where I was on the way to college and when I was almost near to BDS department, I could see my whole class waiting outside the classroom as it was not yet opened by the college housekeeping personnel.

I just joined my classmates. Afterwards Meenu joined me. After a few seconds Meenu gradually said; Deeksha Jack reached Bangalore today morning. Oh is it?!! I asked. After a small pause, Meenu added; Jack called to my mobile number, after getting down at the Bangalore railway station. When I picked Jack call, he just asked about you first. I am really dazed when I heard it.

Even I was amazed to hear that, but I didn't react to her at all. Then, as our classrooms were opened we both went inside the classroom.

It's just 15 minutes left over for our physiology sessions to get started. We all could see a few of our north Indians classmates entering the classroom, but Jack had not come yet. Just 5 minutes before our session Jack entered the classroom. Then our physiology sessions started, without delay.

After an hour or more when the session was over, Jack came and spoke with all our friends. He bought all the things what everyone had asked for from his hometown but he didn't buy anything for me it seems.

At last, I could see Jack coming to my desk while I was copying my notes of previous sessions held. Jack came and sat next to me. Hi Deeksha how you are. And what's up? Jack asked. Hey am fine and nothing special Jack. So, I am back here safely Deeksha, are you happy? I just smiled and said, yes, Jack.

Conjointly, I didn't buy anything for you as per your wish Deeksha. Hey, C'mon Jack! You are safe here and that's enough for this Deeksha. Jack saw my eyes, smiled and asked oh is it?! I too smiled and kept quiet. Okay, let me go to my desk and copy my notes, Jack said. Hey sure Jack, I replied. So he went back to his desk. As days passed by Jack become my close friend as like before. We both had forgotten all our fights.

A few days later, our batch headed for the anatomy sessions bit early. As usual college starts at 9 Am, but our batch was asked to come to anatomy labs straight away by 8am without going to classrooms in the morning. Once I entered the lab, I could see only 3 of my classmates in the lab. I exchanged a few words with them. Also, I saw a big square shaped table in the lab which had been kept for cadaver display.

Slowly, as time flew by almost all students were present in the lab. Girls were asked to stand on one side of the cadaver table and boys vice versa. As few more students are yet to join us, the Professor told we would wait for another 5-10 minutes. Then we would start the session. When I and one more girl were standing near the cadaver display table, Jack came, kept his college bag in the lab and he went out of the lab.

After a few minutes I could feel someone hitting my shoulder gently from behind with his shoulder where I could feel the person breathes and perfume odor. When I rapidly turned back to see who was it? It was Jack.

The moment I saw him, Jack pretended like seeing somewhere and within seconds he went away like nothing has happened. I was shocked as well surprised. I thought why Jack behaved like that? Within a few seconds, the sessions started. Almost after 2 hours we had a break. So everyone sat and started relaxing, as we all were standing almost for more than an hour in the lab.

I and my friend Lalitha sat at a different table while all other girls sat in two other different tables. And some of our class boys were roaming here and there and a few others sat at a separate table. Lalitha just dropped down her head on my lap as she felt so tired.

Suddenly, when we turned towards Jack, we both could realize that; Jack was staring at both of us from a distance. Then he murmured something. When I looked at him with curiosity, I could see a slight smile on his face. And his eyes spoke a thousand words. Jack open your mouth and say it out instead of murmuring, Lalitha said.

I just closed my eyes and waited for him to continue. Hey Lalitha you are lying on Deeksha's lap, Jack said. So what?!! Lalitha asked. Before Jack could reply her, I understood what Jack was about to say. Hence, I smirked and said; Jack well you drop down your head on your table for some time. Even Lalitha understood it. So she said; Jack this is too much okay. I didn't say anything to you Lalitha, Jack said. Then he dropped down his head on his table.

Yes, after 15 minutes of break the anatomy practical sessions again started. As 2nd semester was a break semester we had very less leisure hours. The Physiotherapy department has break semesters, i.e. out of 8 semesters (4 years) 2nd, 4th, 7th and 8th are break semesters for us. The rest of the semesters are carry over. If we fail in break semester, we have to sit at home till we clear it and we won't be able to join our regular batch at all because the regular batch would run before us. So almost there will be a mix up of seniors and juniors in all batches and the exception is 1st year. We always had tight schedules of sessions and everyone started striving hard as no one wants to have a break in their career.

Even my gang had very less interaction between each one of us because whenever we had leisure hours we prepared notes or else we just dropped down our heads on our desks and closed our eyes for some time so that we could feel relaxed. Our days just passed on like that.

And on one fine day when classes were over for that day, everyone was about to leave home. Sayina told she will leave for the day along with my classmate Devaki as she was going alone. By the time I was preparing notes with Meenu and Lalitha. So, I said okay to her.

Afterwards, Jack said hey Deeksha C'mon pack up quickly. Jack again said; Deeksha, I will wait downstairs please come quickly and he left the classroom. Slowly, after 15 minutes when I, Lalitha and Meenu reached downstairs we could see Jack speaking with some of our classmates. Hence, I went to the bike shed along with Meenu and Lalitha. We 3 started speaking about our physiology notes besides Meenu and Lalitha were keeping their college bags on the bike.

In between these Jack came near us. Hey, what you girls were speaking about? Let me know about it so that I can also join the debate girls, Jack said. Nothing Jack, we can leave for the day now, Meenu said. Then I was speaking with my friend Lalitha for a few more minutes. Also, we both could hear Meenu and Jack conversation slightly in between. Their conversation is as follows; hey Meenu won't you tell your friend. Meenu smirked and said, who asked you to see her Jack.

Withal, I and Lalitha couldn't understand anything about their conversation, though we heard it. Jack! Wait for a few more minutes, we three would go to the canteen and buy some water packets as I feel so thirsty, Meenu said. Okay, come back quickly, Jack said. When we 3 are on the way to canteen Meenu said; Deeksha see your churidhar pants it looks so transparent, don't wear it anymore. Also, your churidhar has side cuts so it's visible from your thighs. I am sorry I didn't realize it before, I said.

Say Sorry to Jack because he only noticed it and we were speaking about that only. What?! I asked?!! Then I remember thinking to myself; why Jack always sees me from tip to toe from what chapels I wear up to what hair bands and also how I wear it. Did none of my friends or no one else wear dresses like this in my class? Yes, they wear, but Jack never spot them at all. Then, why me alone? Jack watched all my activities and if something was wrong, he conveyed it to me somehow, but finally when I asked did you love me? Obviously he would have a permanent answer, saying no you are only my friend. Aww!! It's irritating.

By the time we three were back to our bike shed. Meenu smirked at Jack and said conveyed. Ok bye, it's already late for you and Lalitha so leave now, Jack said. Yup, byes!! Will see you tomorrow girls, I said. Deeksha, shall we leave now, Jack asked. I didn't say anything but I walked with him and I felt introverted when I looked at my pants. Then when we reached the Jack hostel entrance, he said bye Deeksha, go safely, see you tomorrow. I said; yup, sure! Bye and left. On my way to the room, I thought mentally, does Jack love me? But I didn't have any answer.

The next day, we had our usual classes in college. During the last leisure hour of that day one of our department professors came to our classroom. The professor asked me to come to our department staff room and he asked the rest of the students to study even in leisure hours as it was a break semester. Then, the professor left to the staff room. I was a bit stunned, petrified and befuddled until I entered my department staff room.

The moment I stepped inside my department staff room, I could see some discussions were going on between all my professors.

And the minute I asked excuse me, all my staffs together said congratulations Deeksha!! Come inside, come! One of my senior professor's said. I was euphoric as well bowled over. And one of my senior professors said, Deeksha take your seat. Once I took my seat, she said; Deeksha your first semester results came and you got university first.

One more student from your batch got university second. We will let you know later who that was because we want to convey it to that student first. We do have graduation award ceremony for whole university this year. So, tomorrow you both go to Engineering department and meet professor Radha as she is the head of organizing committee for this graduation award ceremony program of our university. She would tell what you people should do. Ok ma'am, I said.

My entire professors screamed congrats once again for bringing my department as number one in whole university and they all were really very proud of me. Furthermore, my professors asked me to keep up the good work. Yup, sure, ma'am, I said. Shall I leave now, ma'am? I asked. Sure, the professor said. Really, I felt like I was on cloud nine that moment and I cherish the moment yet.

When I came back to my classroom, I could see the eagerness of all my friends and classmates to know what it was. And why they called me to the staff room. Without more ado, I could hear from a few of my classmates what happen Deeksha? What our professors said to you. Our first semester result has come, I screamed. On top of that, university top is from our department and that too from our batch. Then I screeched; it's me who got university first and it seems university second is also from our department, but they didn't tell me who it was.

The whole batch was happy but after hearing my words, but it was my north Indian classmate Shanwar who told congrats first. Gradually all my classmates wished me. At last! All my friends wished me one by one.

Though my friends were haughty of me they all were tedious as they didn't make it to the top in exams. And my friend Prakash didn't wish me yet. I didn't expect that kind of attitude from all my friends, but I didn't say out anything to them. In between all this, we all saw our classmate Akshara coming out of our department staff room.

Once Akshara reached our classroom, she jumped in joy and said hey guys, yes!! We made it!! University second is also from our batch alone. So, the topper is Deeksha and next it's me Akshara and in another one week there is graduation award ceremony this year for whole university it seems, Akshara screamed in ecstasy. Everyone in class wished Akshara and me one more time.

The next day, both Akshara and I went to the Engineering department of our university to meet graduation ceremony organizing committee head Dr. Radha of the engineering department. Once we reached the upstairs of the engineering department, we both started asking for Professor Dr. Radha as she was unavailable in her room. I t looked like as if, she was busy with the arrangements for the upcoming award ceremony.

Finally, when professor Dr.Radha was about to go downstairs she saw us. Instantaneously she asked; hey you guys are from the Physiotherapy department right? Deeksha and Akshara am I right? I and Akshara were thunderstruck and felt blissful as well swollen with pride because someone from different departments of that university recognized us swiftly.

We both felt it's exactly our top scores which made them to recognize us unerringly. And the organizing committee head asked us to be there near the stage along with other university rank holders on the day of the award ceremony program because the awards will be issued by college chairman, also it would be by department wise, she said. I won't be able to search for everyone on that day, so please come early to the engineering department and we will tell you guys where you should get seated, she said. Then she asked for our mobile numbers.

Finally the professor Dr.Radha said; congrats once again guys, keep up the good work. See you people on the day of the award ceremony. We both said; yup, thank you, ma'am, and for sure we will be on time, on the upcoming award ceremony day. Then, I and Akshara went back to our department.

On the way to our department Akshara said; I am really proud Deeksha, we both should keep up our top marks in second semester also. Yes, we should, I said. After reaching our department, we both met our department professors and gave intimation that we both had met Professor Dr. Radha of the engineering department and then we went back to our classroom.

I told my parents regarding my university top marks. They were so glad and proud as well, but my parents told they couldn't come for graduation ceremony because house modification work was going on in my hometown. Everyone will be here seeing my award receiving ceremony, but the most important people of my lives were not able to come down here, I said. After hearing those words from me, my father said ok I will come down dear, but straight away to college by evening and mom won't be able to make it because she should be here in hometown as work can't be stopped. Ok dad! See you on the award function day, bye for now, I said and I hung up.

Next, we got circular from college management regarding award ceremony program. The circular conveyed all the students should attend the program by evening 5 pm the next week. And there would be no classes for the day. Afterwards, our gang decided to gather in college by afternoon on the award ceremony program day as we all can have fun altogether before the program starts. At length, the most awaited award ceremony day has come.

By afternoon around 2 pm my gang gathered in college near our department and we all sat together in steps as Prakash and Kiran are yet to come.

The instant, Prakash and Kiran arrived, we all walked towards the program stage, which was next to the engineering department and on our way, and we all could see Kiran and Divakar kidding Jack. Hey Jack, who suggested you wear the casual's man that too a

T-shirt with collar, Kiran and Divakar asked. Why it's not looking good for me? Jack said. Then everyone in gang broke into laughter and said; hey, if you don't mistake us, you look good in formals than casuals' man.

Immediately, Jack said; hey you guys then wait outside my hostel entrance or else you guys wait in the engineering department canteen which is next to the boy's hostel. I will just go to the hostel, change my dress and for sure I will join you guys quickly. Then Jack left to the hostel.

Hey, you guys will never keep hushed or what? Prakash asked all my friends. Why you told Jack like that? You all must have said that he looked better in casuals. See, now how long he was taking to come back. Divakar and Kiran chuckled. They both said who knew machi, Jack will take this long.

Slowly each one in my gang started saying; hey, someone call to Jack mobile number and ask him to come out of hostel soon, as it's already getting late. After 2 to 3 calls Jack came out of his hostel in formals and he looked much better than before. Then we all went and sat near the arts and the science department stadium, which was almost close to the award ceremony stage as well near to the engineering department.

We could see students from all departments roaming here and there and some were getting ready to inauguration programs. Someone from my gang started asking, did our department participate in any program. Then a few friends from my gang said; yes, I heard some of our seniors were.

We had enjoyed ourselves very much the day. Jack was with me. The whole gang was together and we had lots of fun. I felt like I was complete. I had good friends to fall back on, my love and the college life I always wanted. In the past few hours, we all had lived and felt every small moment we had gone through. All of a sudden Sonia screamed; Jack what happened?!! Where you get injured? Abruptly everyone from our gang turned their eyes towards Jack and we all could see a big bandage in one of his toe fingers. Jack said, hey guys, it's just a small injury only and before he could say how he got injured, our classmate Akshara came down and said; hey Deeksha come, all university top rank holders were asked to come near the stage.

Yes, within a few seconds, we all could hear the same announcement from the stage.Before we both could leave, all my friends said; hey, we are really happy for you guys and just for your info, our department would be seated in the last few rows from right side of the stage including our professors. They added; we all would gather there. So, after receiving your awards don't search for us, come straight away to last few rows.

We both said ok and started walking towards the stage. Then all toppers were asked to get seated near to stage in the first few rows and followed by their parents and all departments of university one by one. When the program was about to start my father came down and then Akshara father. I and my father got introduced by Akshara, to her father. Then both our fathers sat together. And once I and Akshara stepped on stage one by one to receive our awards we both could hear a big round of non-stop applause from our department.

After receiving our awards we went right away to our professors. One more time, we heard congrats from them. Also, we both heard congrats from students of our department as well from students of other departments too. Then our professors asked both of us to meet our department principle with our parents.They said our principle would be sitting somewhere in the front rows.

Eventually, I and Akshara with our parents met our Principal. Our principal said congrats to both of us. The principal said to our Parents, that they were really proud to have me and Akshara in their department. She added; the reason why I asked you both to meet me was, I want you guys to hold this topper rank not only in next semester, but till the end semester and I would be expecting that from both of you. Yup, sure, ma'am, we both said. Then she said to both our parents; nice meeting you and she left. Then Akshara and her father said bye and left. I asked my father to go to my cousin home as it would take a little more time for me to come to room as I want to bid bye to all my friends. Ok, come quickly my father said and he left college. Afterwards I went in search for my friends and I could see everyone near boy's hostel entrance along with Meenu school friends.

Meenu introduced me to all her school friends. Then, my friends asked me; what our principal had told and when I conveyed it; Jack asked; what we are here since then, if you both alone should stay at the top ranks. I was dreary as well become quiet after hearing those words from Jack. Anyhow, I have to leave now, bye everyone. See you all tomorrow in college, I said and left college.

I reached my room by 9pm with my dad as I went directly to my cousin's house from college. I had a long time conversation with my cousin and her family member's about the gratifying moments of my award ceremony program in college.

Next, I could see Jack name popping up on my mobile screen and when I picked the call, Deeksha just wait for a few minutes, Jack said. Then, I could hear; hey sorry Deeksha!! I was powdering my wound with some medicines that's why. I thought, it would take time for you to pick the call so I started powdering my wound, but you picked up the call swiftly.

Anyways, I need your physiology book tomorrow as you have different author. Okay, I will bring it tomorrow and how is your wound Jack, I said. He was hushed for a few seconds, but after that, his retort left me bemused. Jack retort to me was; Deeksha, I knew Jack is not your first precedence, you didn't ask me about it when you saw me at college. Hey, C'mon Jack I didn't notice it at after all, I said. Jack instantly hollered; Yes!! I know it, because you didn't care for me now-a –days and he hung up the phone without saying anything about his wound.

Again, I spoke mentally, why this Jack is so possessive of me alone? Why not on my other friends? Why he wants only me to observe him from tip to toe, ie. From his hairstyle to dressing style, the shoes he wear and whether his health and mood are fine. But ultimately Jack would say, I am just her friend alone and not anything more than that.

Suddenly, I could hear my dad voice who was it? Come and sleep its already late and don't be there in the balcony for a long time, dad said. Yup, it was Jack dad and he asked for my Physiology book, I said. Ok, come and sleep now, Dad said. Within seconds I went to bed otherwise my dad will scold me. Finally, Jack never ever told about that wound to me even in college on further days. As I got fed off, I just left without asking Jack about it.

As days passed by, on a witty day in college, when I was chit chatting with my friends Meenu, Lalitha and a few more in lunch break. All of a sudden, one of my friend started saying; guys, after 10 years from now think how we all would be. Hey, we all would have married and would have kids by that time. By the same token, life would be utterly different for each one of us, by the time, all my friends said.

Exactly! And I would have got married to Jack by that time, I said. Instantly both my close friends became furious and asked what?! Come again, please!! I just muttered, oh my God! Why do I say about this now!!

Then there was a silence of the air. Gradually both my friends asked me; Deeksha, you told you won't love Jack any more on that day, after our advice. Then what you told us was a lie? I kept quiet for some time, and then I replied no! It's not like that. I was not able to tell you guys on that day that I couldn't even imagine a life without Jack. I felt, I can convey it to both of you when Jack accepts his love for me.

All my friends kept unperturbed for a few seconds. Then all of a sudden my close friends Meenu and Lalitha told; we trusted you a lot on this matter and now it was not true. As soon as Jack came back from lunch, they went ahead and said to Jack about this.

Immediately Jack came to my desk and said; Deeksha, I want to speak with you for a few minutes. It's a leisure hour for us and apart from me; no one else was sitting on my desk. All my classmates were roaming here and there in the classroom and somewhere chit chatting. So I said, yes, you can speak to me now and here itself Jack. Jack was stifled for a few seconds.

Afterwards, Jack asked, Deeksha whatever I heard is true?!! What you heard Jack?!! I asked. Did you say you still love me and you hope I love you too?! Yes!! Whatever you heard was true Jack, I said. Jack was stunned after hearing my words. Why do you love me such madly and why you are like this?!! Jack asked.

After a small pause, Jack again said; you would have heard through Meenu that one of my hostel friends Dhilip asked me to say straight away like this. I don't love you and whatever you want to do, you do Deeksha and I didn't care or bother about it. But I never want to say like that to you Deeksha because I want all my friends to be happy. If it's someone else, right away I would have said like that.

Instantaneously I said; I know very well that you love me but you are hiding it from me. Isn't it Jack?! Hey, Deeksha, I didn't feel anything like that. Ok Deeksha! Let me explain like this to you, Jack said. Then we both could see our friend Prakash coming to my desk. The minute Prakash reached my desk, Jack said; hey Prakash, we are speaking about something important da! So don't disturb us both for a few more minutes. Prakash understood, chortled and he said ok ok machi you continue. Then he left the place.

Jack started explaining me again, hey Deeksha think in this way, suppose! Jack insisted me again that he was saying only suppose. I am (Jack) saying I love you. Did you think what will happen after this 4 and half years? The truth is we have been walking parallel to each other and will end up taking different paths during our life journey, especially after our college life. If that happens won't you cry Deeksha? I know for sure you will cry more by that time, but it would be of no use. So you cry now itself Deeksha and I feel that would be much better, Jack said.

I interrupted instantly and said, do not be imaginary, how come you know that my path would be different from yours Jack. Yet you don't know utterly about me. Jack interrupted and said; might be!! But Deeksha, I know very well about my family and my career ahead. So, I think it's better for you to cry now for this because your Jack didn't love you. He is thinking you only as his close friend that's it!! Okay?!! Better you don't talk to me if you have this thought in your mind anymore, Jack said.

I became furious on hearing Jack's words. So, I said; better don't ever have an imaginary thought about the others life path or future ahead Jack, though he/she might be your friend. Furthermore, don't ever think a girl from a small town won't have a career path like you.

Conjointly, I think it's better to clear out this issue right now Jack because this thought never allows me to concentrate on my studies and for nature's sake, I just came in to this magnificent university only for that and not for love, romance or friendship. Above all, I am just lucky to get such good friends who care about my future, family and career too. I knew, you are one among my good friends and that's why you are explaining me to this extent.

Jack, I don't want to miss my friends for any reason. Friendship is entirely different from love and I know that very well too. But love happens naturally. I never knew why I love you alone, such madly though there were so many other boys not only in our friend's gang but also in this class/department/university. My first crush is only you. I am lucky as like our friend Lalitha words.

My first crush is my love. So I just want to let you know that, I am madly in love with you and I don't know what you think of me, but you are really very special for me. If only you could hear my heart's voice you would have known that I will love you like no one else. I want you to stay by my side. I love you so much that I cannot express enough. So, what about you Jack? You really don't love me?

After a small pause, I asked; Jack is it something else that is stopping you?! Jack was hushed and he didn't answer me. At length, I said;

what I want to tell you is; Jack, it's your wish to love me or not. But you don't have any rights to say; Deeksha, you should not love Jack because it's Deeksha wish alone.

Deeksha likes you; she feels you are the special person in her life. After all, Deeksha loves you and she feels Jack loves her too. If Jack doesn't feel anything like that, it's fine. Jack got up from the desk instantly after hearing my words.

Jack said; ok Deeksha!! If you just want to do what you feel like and not listen to what I have to say, then get lost!! I am leaving. And one more request to you from today, you don't talk to me anymore, Jack said. Fine, I won't ever disturb you again. But before leaving just tell me one thing Jack-do you seriously not love me? In my heart, I had really wanted him to say yes, I miss you, I want you, and I am all yours. But Jack had unfortunately said, no, I don't. I do not even care for you now Deeksha!!

Even if we cross paths in the future, I will try my level best to be indifferent and that's final Jack, I said. Then Jack went back to his desk.

And it's just 5 more minutes left out for the leisure hour to get over. After that, our sessions started. So, it's almost the end of the day and everyone started leaving for home. My friends Sayina and Jack didn't call me. They both left the classroom, when I was wadding my college bag with my books. Then I just started leaving for home alone as well forlorn. On my way, I saw all my friends in the bike shed including Jack and Sayina.

When I went to speak with Meenu, instantly Sayina, Deepika and Lalitha said bye to everyone barring me and left for home. Divakar and Prakash started walking gradually towards Jack hostel and they both kept on saying, Jack come swiftly;

Besides these I could hear Meenu words; don't talk to us Deeksha as you have broken our trust which we had on you. Especially as a friend?! How can we believe you again! Meenu added; however, it takes only one second to break someone's trust, but it takes an entire lifetime to rebuild it Deeksha. For God sake, Deeksha please realize this is just infatuation and it's not love, Jack said.

Without ado I said; I didn't speak with you anymore Jack and this feeling is never infatuation it's called love. After a small pause, I said; Jack I deserve better than that. What was my fault? One day you are going to wake up and realize how much I loved you, but I will not be your side by that time. Jack didn't speak anything after hearing those words from me.

Divakar and Prakash were watching all those conversations standing at a distance with their mouth open as like some movie shooting was going on but they kept on saying, Jack come we will leave from here. At long last I said; if it was my fault then let me walk away from you all. I thought our friendship would last forever, but now it's time to walk away. Then I left for home immediately.

On my way to home, I felt; there comes a time in life when we realize that we cannot force love, respect or friendship. If it's not from the heart, then it's false and meaningless. We cannot beg someone to stay in our lives if they want to leave. May be I don't deserve to be his girlfriend. Jack loved me. He really did. I hope he did. Is it the end of everything? Is it the end of happiness? End of our friendship. End of our relationship?

I had realized that our friendship could never be the same again. But to accept things as they were is never easy. To accept reality is a challenge. But life brings you to a stage where you need to accept the hardest of the truths and move on for those who still love you and want you in their lives. Then I remember thinking to myself, trust me Jack, I am still crazy about you. Whenever I see you, my heart still skips a beat. But nobody was there to hear me. Hence, I cried my heart out. Sometimes, we need pain and heartache to see what matters most. No one can understand our pain until they are put in our position.

From next day onwards I was lonely in college. I started having my lunch alone in the classroom and sat with my other classmates in anatomy and physiology labs for practical sessions.

I missed my friends everywhere. I stopped going to the canteen. Whenever I went there, I could see that table where we all used to sit. Everything seemed to be different. Though I felt I just wanted to avoid everyone, I was missing them badly. I was regretting my decision.

I felt; Mistakes make us realize that sometimes there are no time outs and no second chance. I was utterly down in the dumps where all my other classmates could realize that something went wrong between me and my friends, but none of them came and asked what it was as it was among our friends.

As I was utterly dismal, my friends were scared about me. Hence, they informed everything (whatever had happened among our friends) to my parents. Therefore, my parents asked me to take leave for 2 days and to come hometown as I could feel unperturbed.

The next day morning I just applied leave to college for 2 days and started travelling to my hometown. Suddenly I reminisced; it was Jack birthday on that day. So after reaching my home town I decided to call him as well, I realized; strange are our emotions. Even when things won't go our way, we still take a chance.

Once I reached my hometown, I just crossed the bus stop and went to a nearby STD booth. I knew none of my friends would pick my call if I dial from my mobile number. Also, I didn't have Jack's new mobile number. Therefore, I just dialed in Meenu number from STD booth. Once Meenu picked my call she recognized my voice. So she asked what?!! Deeksha. I want to wish Jack, can you give the mobile to him, please!!

Immediately I could hear Meenu strident background voice, which said; Hey, Jack, Deeksha is on call!! It seems she wants to wish you!! Besides, I could hear all my friends' chit chatting voices. In the background, I heard Jack boisterous voice, which said; No Meenu, I don't want to speak with Deeksha. So, after a long wait, Meenu said; hope you would have heard the response from Jack. Then, she hung up right away.

I was about to snivel, but I gave money and came out of the phone booth. I felt, no one cared about me; they all were having bountiful joy. The best thing about the worst time of our life is that we get to see the truth behind everyone we have cared for. I realized it. Also, I could sense, I was moving towards a slow and painful death i.e. death of friendship, love and the bonding. Then from the bus stop, I started walking towards my home.

After walking for 10 minutes, I suddenly realized I was going in the opposite direction of my home. I couldn't control myself from sobbing. My tears rolled down my cheeks instantaneously. Then I started walking back towards the bus stop. On my way, I spoke mentally, I am staying here in my home town from my birth for nearly 19 years, but how come I missed the way to my home. That's all, life is all about?

 The moment, I reached back bus stop, I dialed my dad number and asked him to come and pick me up at the bus stop. And while waiting for my dad, again I spoke mentally, Jack is this infatuation man? If it's an infatuation, will I think or take it deep to the heart. No way! It's pure love and that made me to call you on your birthday though you hurt me very badly.

You won't understand about true love Jack because you never knew what true love is all about. I felt, life is so strange, sometimes it gives us so much that we don't know, how to handle it and sometimes it takes away all that it gave us in the same breath. Meanwhile I could see my father coming at a distance to pick me up. I murmured, No, I don't love Jack. I don't want him back. But the fact was, I was just fooling myself. I had always loved and cared for Jack. Why did I love Jack so much? I had no answer to that. I still wondered why I let him go.

Next, I was utterly hassle-free at home for 2 days after my father advice. I reached Bangalore next day morning. In college, I never spoke to any one of my friends. I was hushed and I kept concentrating on studies, especially on my weaker subjects. I joined a few of my classmates and started preparing for my practical sessions. By the time Kiran was the only person among my friends who talked to me as well with my whole gang. I started concentrating on my studies, though I was not able to. I remember thinking to myself; someone once said that death is not the greatest loss in life. The greatest loss is what dies inside us while we are alive.

As days went by, on one fine day in college when we had the leisure time for whole afternoon I sat alone in the first floor balcony with my physiology books to study. Also, I could see a few of my other classmates who did the same, by the time.

Kiran came to me and asked; Deeksha, I have some doubts about Physiology previous sessions. Can you explain it to me now? Yes, I can, but come with your books I will explain it. Afterwards, Kiran came with his books and sat next to me. Then we both could see our classmate Shanwar coming towards us.

Hey guy's as it's my birthday today I arranged for a small birthday party in my room so both you are invited. All our classmates are coming, so you both join them, Shanwar said. Okay!! I am coming, Kiran said. Jack and Shanwar are roommates. So, I said; I am sorry Shanwar I won't be able to come. I hope you can understand my situation. Hey, it's my room too and I am inviting you for my birthday party so you should come. Come along with all our classmates Deeksha, Shanwar said.

I never want to go to Jack room, but I didn't know what I should say to Shanwar. After hearing both our conversations, Kiran said; Hey, leave if she doesn't want to come. And you know the reason right? Shanwar. Yup!! I know, but it's my birthday party and not Jack's, Shanwar said. After a few seconds, Shanwar said; Ok Deeksha!! It's fine, no problem, Shanwar said. Then, Shanwar left back to the classroom. And when I was about to start clarifying Kiran's Physiology doubts, he said; Deeksha think about your semester exams as it's very nearby. And don't ever forget that this is a break semester.

If you are gloomy and not concentrating on your studies, it will be very difficult to pass your exams, this time. You are University topper in first semester, if you are not able to get the top position this time at least try to pass this semester otherwise what our professors and everyone will think about you. C'mon, it's about your career and future ahead. I hope you will be aware of it. Ok Kiran, I can understand. For sure, I will try to focus on my studies alone from now onwards, I said.

At the end of the day, when I was about to leave for home, a few of my classmates who doesn't know the way to Shanwar room asked me to wait for a few minutes, so they join me, up to the Shanwar room as it's very nearby to my room. At last, when we all were very near to Shanwar room, I showed them the way and said bye guys. You are not coming to birthday party Deeksha?! A few of my classmates asked. No! I will go to my room and then I will come. You guys carry on!! I said. Oh!! Ok Deeksha. Anyways, come soon; see you there, bye Deeksha. Then they all left to Shanwar room.

After reaching my room, I thought about my friend Kiran words. Then, I started thinking deeply about my break semester and my exam plans. Yes, as usual, I was left alone in college the next day. Once the classes were over for that day and when I was about to leave for home, I could hear Kiran voice from behind. Hey, Deeksha wait, I would join you as I am coming to a bus stop which was on the way to your room, Kiran said. Yup!! Come quickly Kiran, I said. Deeksha, I already wagged my college bag with my books, but I was simply kidding our classmate Priyanka, so it was late, Kiran said. Oh!! Ok!! I said with a smile on my face.

Then, we both started walking slowly. On our way we both were speaking about something. All of a sudden, Kiran asked; hey Deeksha shall I say something? Yup!! Sure, why not? I said. None of your problems and friends, even your close friends Meenu and Lalitha was going to come with you till the end of your life.

Only your studies and your parents until they are alive are going to come with you till the end. If you have a career, you can have a good life. So, please concentrate on your studies and remember it's a break semester not a carry over. I will wish to say a few more words to you Deeksha. I said; yes, sure Kiran! After a few years, we all would be somewhere. On one fine day, wherever Jack was, for sure he will think he had missed you. Jack would also think, Deeksha proposed me on that day itself, but why I didn't accept her love. I missed her. I must have married her and not this one. Kiran again said, for sure Deeksha!! He will think it in this way on one day, regardless of wherever Jack might be. Kiran added; what I would say is Jack is unlucky, that's why he missed a nice girl like you from his life.

I interrupted instantaneously and said; no Kiran, it's me who is unlucky. I am trying hard to forget him. But I couldn't. Today I think in this way; if I had not liked him, I would not have loved him. If I would not have loved him, I would not have missed him. Kiran said; never think like that Deeksha. And by the time, we reached the bus stop. Hence Kiran waved bye to me and left.

Jack never looked back even though I was still waiting for him. My heart said Jack would come back, but I knew I should trust my mind. After reaching my room, I thought about my friend Kiran words once again. Whatever Kiran said was true, only my studies were going to come with me till my end. I wanted to take a different path from now on. So, I decided to concentrate on my studies alone to forget everything else happened. Also, I smiled and thought that things need to come to an end if they have to make way for a beautiful beginning.

After that, gradually I felt hassle-free from memories of Jack and my friends. I started concentrating on my studies. Next, once I laid a study plan for my 2nd semester exams, I realized I won't be able to reach top position that time, but at least I can pass that time without keeping a break in my career. For that, I should strive hard from that minute as I had so many portions left out to complete, for my exams.

The next day in college when I had a leisure hour, I started preparing for my exams as per my study plan. I could see all my friends were enjoying like before and they never cared about me. Then, I said to myself; even I don't care about you guys, why should I? Above all, I felt most friendships only last for a particular phase of life.

After a few minutes, one of my classmates named Sunilkumar came towards me to first floor balcony where I sat to prepare notes. Hey Deeksha, Kiran asked me to convey these words to you; don't mistake Kiran's words regarding your studies. Kiran doesn't want any good student to lose their studies despite of any reasons and that's why he advised you being your friend. Hey, there is nothing wrong in it, Sunil. Actually, I should thank him for his advice, I said.

Anyways, Kiran felt, you might mistake him. Hence he conveyed it through me Deeksha. That's fine, no problem Sunil, I said. Okay!! You continue preparing your notes; I am getting back to classroom, Sunil said. Yup, thank you, Sunil, I said. After that, I wanted to forget every fight I had with Jack and that was the time I decided to take some firm decisions in my life. To boot with, I thought why I should try holding on to the past when the future can be so much better.

As the days flew by, our batch had our 2nd semester model exams and we got our study holidays too. That time we all were asked to collect the no due certificates as well as the hall tickets on same day morning but hall ticket would be issued in university office for all departments of the university which was near engineering department. And the hall ticket issuing date would be notified for each one, from college through the phone.

Before my 2nd semester model exams, I could see Lalitha and Deepika having lunch separately and the rest of my gang together. I felt, there would again be some problem between these guys, so it seems they were not speaking. Anyways, I had been ignoring all my friends for the last few days. I realized they don't deserve my friendship. Time changes everything. After all, I thought it's none of my business. I was as usual speaking with everyone in the classroom, including my friend Kiran.

When I came back to my senses, I realized, it was exam time again. I wanted to study well and secure good marks. The second half of the year is always dangerous than the first half of the year. I prepared hard enough for my exams and I didn't know about anyone else preparations as I didn't speak to anyone else in my study holidays.

Finally, the day had come for collecting exam hall tickets. I reached earlier to college to collect my exam hall tickets. The whole batch was asked to fill in the no due certificates and hand it over to our class representative. While filling those forms I had some doubts regarding my semester fee paid structure as I had requested the college management to convert my first year hostel fees in to 2nd semester fees.

Also, I paid the rest of the semester fees amount, but the record says that hostel fees had not been transferred as semester fees yet though I got the information from my principal that it had been changed at the beginning of that semester. Hence, I asked Kiran, what I should do. Wait, I will ask Jack to clarify it with our professors as he was the class representative of our batch, Kiran said. Jack was unperturbed when Kiran conveyed the message.

Jack continued collecting filled in no due forms from my batch mates, but I was still waiting for his reply. So, I asked Kiran one more time about it. And Kiran went ahead and asked the same to Jack. I won't be able to go and ask for anyone personally, I can only give the common instructions for everyone, if it's their problem they only should go ahead, Jack said stridently, callously as well instantly looking at my face. Kiran was hushed. I became furious after getting such a reply from Jack. I started walking towards Principal room instantaneously. I spoke mentally, who asked this fool to go and ask for me personally, then what for he is elected as representative for this batch? Also, I thought, times had changed. Relationships had changed. Love had disappeared. Meanwhile, I had reached my Principal room entrance. Yes, Come in Deeksha, Principal said.

My Principal always had a good impression on me apart from all other students of my batch as I scored University top in first semester. Principal, spoke with college management regarding my semester fee issue. Then, Principal asked me to go to the university office, meet Mr.Ravichander and bring a no due form from him so that she can sign and give it to me. Principal, added; then you can go and collect your hall ticket at university office. Sure, thank you, ma'm, I said. And I started walking to the university office.

On my way, I remember thinking myself, oh my god!! Again, I should walk back this 1 kilometer and should get back again to the university office. What a day for you Deeksha!! For receiving your exam hall ticket itself, you are suffering to this extent. I don't know how you are going to write your exams!!

The moment I reached the university office, which was near the engineering department, I came back to my senses. Once I got my no due form at university office, I came out of the office and I could see all my classmates were waiting outside the university office to collect hall tickets as they had already completed their no due formalities exception is Jack and Meenu because Jack has to hand over the completed no due forms of our batch in principal room being a representative. Then, we all could hear an announcement from university office, which said; First year physiotherapy department, please wait for 15 more minutes.

Once we finish issuing hall tickets for the dental department, we will start with yours. After hearing it, I thought I should join back my batch swiftly at university office. So I started walking rapidly towards my department with my no due form and when I was almost near to Principal room, I saw Jack and Meenu walking towards the university office to join our batch.

The moment I crossed Jack, he asked; hey everything alright? Deeksha. I didn't reply to Jack, but kept on walking towards the principal room thinking that hall ticket would not have been issued yet for my batch at university office and that's why these guys were walking slowly. I should get signature instantly from the principal in my no due form and should get back to university office as soon as possible. Yes, at last, I got a clearance certificate from my principal. Then, the principal told, she would speak to the university office Deeksha. You can go and get your hall ticket along with your classmates, the principal said. Principal added; Deeksha All the best for your exams, do well, we all were expecting more from you at your exams.

I smiled, nodded my head and said yup sure Ma'm. I will do my best and thank you so much for your timely help. Then, I walked back quickly to my university office. I could see the first student from my batch entering the university office to receive her hall ticket. I went and stood fourth in line as per attendance register order.

I was blissful because ultimately I received my hall ticket along with my other classmates after a bit struggle. Then I remember thinking to myself; I hate you badly Jack and you had done it wontedly and that's why it took a long time. I really hate you man for your behavior today. Afterwards, I left for my room.

Yes, at long last, our most awaited theory exams started. The paper was extremely tough, but I tried to answer as many questions as I could. Then, one by one all of us trickled out of the classroom. I knew, I won't get top marks that time, but at least I would pass and that's sure. Also, I could hear from all my other classmates, the question paper was not that easy. So let's see what happens. And our practical exams were not yet over. Therefore everyone started preparing for it.

My batch had been split into two groups for practical exams. So, our first batch, which consisted of 18 members, had our practical sessions on the first day. I and my friends Deepu, Lalitha, Kiran, Divakar and Meenu were there in the first batch. Divakar had not arrived to college yet. I went earlier and I stood outside the anatomy lab and was going through my books. Meanwhile I could see Deepu and Lalitha coming towards the lab. They both came near me and said hi Deeksha.

I felt, a lost or broken friendship hurts, but what hurts more was the realization that they weren't a true friend to begin with. Anyways, I don't want to make them feel awful. Also, I want to concentrate on my studies alone. Hence I said; hey hi guys and gazed back at my books. Then, they both went and sat near 2nd floor steps and started preparing separately for practical exams.

By the time, I could see Meenu standing with her books at a distance and Jack was there with her. Though Jack doesn't have an exam on that day as he was in 2nd batch, it seems he just came down to see how everyone was doing and what questions the internal and external examiner were asking, so that he could get an idea for his tomorrow practical exams.

Meanwhile I could hear my name being called by external examiners and when I was about to get into the lab, Divakar came in a hurry and asked hey Deeksha are you going in now? Yup!! Divakar, I said. Hey Deeksha All the best!! Get in soon, Divakar said; with a big smile on his face. I smiled and went inside to the external examiner, but as my previous classmate had not finished yet, I was asked to attend the internal examiner first and later the external examiner. My viva's had gone very well.

Finally, somehow all the 2nd semester exams both theory and practical exams were over. I felt, I will clear the exams this time for sure, but impossible to score top marks. I can't believe it's the end of one year in physiotherapy and we would be promoted to the second year.

Once my semester holidays were announced I left for my hometown happily. I was stress-free and my only thought was on my career and family. Never thought about my friends or Jack love.

My lifestyle, my likes and dislikes everything had changed and so had my behavior along. Because I felt, God had some different plans in mind and I had to my peace with that. A month had gone so soon and college was about to reopen the next week. So I reached back to Bangalore a day prior to the college reopening day. I loved my days in Bangalore. I thought about my parents and the freedom they had given to me. I felt, I should never misuse it at any time in my life.

Chapter 3

It's beginning of the 3rd semester. As usual going to college was not an exciting thought at all after I scuffled with my friends, but there was no other option. The whole first year batch including north Indians had come down to college. We all sat in the old first year classroom and started chit chatting.

After a few minutes one of our professors came to our classroom and said; your classroom has been changed, it's the 2nd classroom from our department staff room in same 1st floor. So your batch can move there now because this classroom is for your juniors that's new joiners. Everyone, especially our batch boys, was fervent to know how many students had joined, especially number of girls. Hence our class boys asked the professor; how many students are joining this time, sir, and when is our junior inauguration program? Our Professor smiled and said we will let you know all this info later. So, C'mon, you guys leave swiftly to your new classroom.

Yes, again, it's desk allocation time in the new classroom. Each one sat according to their wish with their friends. I sat in the first desk in the first row. Suddenly Lalitha and Deepu came and asked; Deeksha shall we occupy your desk. I couldn't say anything because 3 can sit at a desk. Though I kept quiet, they both occupied the same desk along with me. And to my surprise, I could see Meenu, Jack and Sayina occupied the first desk of the second row. I thought, oh!! No!! We all are going to sit in a parallel row!! God!! It's irksome.

Abruptly we all could see a new professor entering our classroom and the professor had given an introduction session. The professor said; she was from dental department and she would be taking microbiology that semester for physiotherapy department.

The third semester had 5 subjects and we had 5 professors from different colleges as well from different departments of the same university, but none of them is from our own department, thus we all were hassle-free.

I felt, I should not get back close to Lalitha and Deepu because they are the same old friends and not new ones.Though I spoke to them, I was never close to them as like before.

As days went by, a big problem arose among my whole gang it seems and they all were separated. Meenu and Jack were together. Divakar was close to Prakash and Somesh and Divakar never spoke with Meenu. Prakash never spoke with Somesh and Jack. Shamili and Sonia were close as they both were staying in college hostel and they spoke with everyone in the gang. Lalitha, Deepu & Sayina were together and they never spoke with Meenu and Jack. Kiran was never close to anyone in the gang, but he spoke to everyone in the gang.

I never asked any of my friends what's the problem about and why everyone in the gang was separated as I felt I never want to know it.

Slowly as the days went by Lalitha, Deepu and I became close, forgetting all our fights. Also, my friend Sayina was close to 3 of us, but she became too close with our classmate Devaki. Furthermore Kiran was too close with our classmate Sunilkumar.

Nearly, after a month, on one fine day at about 11 am morning in the college, we all were chit chatting here and there. All of a sudden, we could hear from one of our department senior that our 2nd semester results were declared. The senior added; the exam results were declared on our college website as usual. Go and check it. After hearing that, there was pin drop silence in the classroom.

Then my classmates Divakar and Jack said; Guys!! We both would go and ask permission from professors to go out & check our results, as we should check from some internet Centre's from outside the college it seems. So, don't worry, we would keep you updated, but please be here in the classroom. We both would call to our classmates Monashka and Meenu mobiles to update the results, they both said and left.

After knowing our second semester results were declared, everyone was terrified about our results. Moreover, Divakar and Jack didn't call anyone yet. So few of my classmates kept on saying why these guys didn't call us yet.

Nearly after 2 hours, our classmates, Jack & Divakar came with the results print out and they both entered the classroom without saying anything. Divakar went and sat in his desk. Once Jack kept the result sheet print out on his table, everyone ran to his table to see it.

As result printout sheet was on Jack table, I went at a snail's pace. I couldn't see the sheet as it's surrounded by my classmates. So I asked one of my classmates to see my results. The person whom I asked doesn't answer me, but for all of a sudden, Jack said hey Deeksha you passed, in a languid tone. I was hushed after hearing it but still stood there.

Though Jack was holding the results sheet yet, the minute everyone left Jack's table, I went and checked the results but Jack was tranquil. I was stunned as well startled after seeing the 2nd semester results because more than half of my classmates were failed. And the problem was it was a break semester. So those failed will lose a semester. They can't continue with us anymore, they have to sit at home for six months. When we write our 3rd semester exams those guys would write their left out subjects of 2nd semester. Then, they would be coming a semester behind us as well just a semester prior to our immediate junior batch. At last, our batch was broken, which was unforeseen.

Everyone sat in their desk silently for nearly half an hour and the class had a pin drop silence. Each one was gloomy and it was a pathetic situation. Even those who passed the break semester never had heart to celebrate it because we felt doleful for our classmates. A few started howling too. Slowly we all could hear a voice which said why it happened like this and it was none other than Divakar's. Everyone remained hushed. So, those failed have to leave for home without more ado. Therefore, Malvika started saying bye and congrats to those who passed. Then Shamile, then Rakesh, Saleem and slowly everyone in the batch who had failed, said bye and congrats to those who passed.

We guys who passed never want them to leave us as well we never want to bid bye. We all kept quiet. My classmate Rakesh sat again on a desk for a few more seconds. He was dejected.

At long last, Rakesh stood up and said, it had happened and nothing can be done for it. Rakesh added; Saleem come, let us leave for home. Then we all could see Saleem sitting at the last desk of classroom. Saleem was wordless.

Really, it was a poignant moment. Felt execrable to see everyone especially Rakesh and Saleem like that because they always keep on making fun in our leisure hours. They make everyone chortle always. From the time we all were together, we had never seen both of them that sad. Finally, all those who failed left the classroom. Once they all left the classroom, it looked so empty and it had pin drop silence with all gloomy faces. It's around 23 students who passed out of 43 altogether.

Afterwards, Divakar said; does it look like a classroom? Never! What is this? Why it happened like this? Why the management failed these many students? No one had any answers because we have not got our marks yet. Who knows even we would have passed scoring border marks. Finally, it was lunch time, but no one wished to have lunch. Slowly, Divakar got up from his desk and asked Prakash, Somesh, Jack to come for lunch with him. Also, he asked the rest of our batch mates to have our lunch. Gradually we all had our lunch.

After lunch when we all were back in the classroom, few of our batch mates said; even we all should be more careful in our upcoming break semesters. We should do well or else the management can do the same for us too. And guys, that's the fact too.

Slowly as the days flew by our 3ʳᵈ semester classes started. My friends Lalitha, Deepika, Sayina & I became close friends again. We never thought about our past friendship and fights. It was really fun days for all four of us.

At long last, it was 8ᵗʰ March 2006 and yes the women's day celebration came. As my room had nearby flower shops my classmates asked me to buy bundles of red roses. So, on March 8ᵗʰ 2006 morning, I reached my college campus prior to my usual time. When I was near to my 3ʳᵈ semester classroom, I could see Jack standing outside our classroom i.e., in the balcony.

The moment Jack saw me with bundle of red roses, he pretended like he was seeing somewhere, but he stood unperturbed in the same place for some time. Then when I was very near to my classroom entrance, Jack went hastily inside the classroom.

The moment, I saw that I couldn't control my smile. I kept walking towards the classroom with a big smile on my face. Once I entered my classroom, I walked towards Jack. Jack was flabbergasted stunned and stood like a statue there, with a hesitation on his face. But Jack doesn't know, my classmate Priyodhani was coming behind him just to collect the roses from me.

I crossed Jack with a wide smile on my face. As soon as I crossed him, Jack was bewildered and he turned instantaneously towards me, to see where I was going. The moment, I gave the bundle of red roses to my classmate Priyodhani, Jack was at ease and he left the place instantly.

Then I remember thinking to myself; hey Jack you thought I just came with red roses to propose you right?! I knew you expected it from me Jack. Even I felt how nice it would be if I do that, but before your heart accepts your love for me leaving besides everything and everyone, I will never do it Jack.

I came back to my senses, once I heard Lalitha and Deepu's voice which said; Deeksha come, let's move for women's day celebration. I suddenly stood up from my desk with a cute smile on my face and said come let's move. The women's day celebration went awesome. I have no words to explain it.

The 3rd semester memories will never allow me to forget my lunch timings were all four friends used to have hotel, lunch apart from our home lunch in a single plate. Also, I can never forget our hassle-free walking minutes after lunch in our university campus and the fun which we had while teasing other departments and the interactions which we had with other department students and with our seniors of our own department.

I feel, I have been there in college yet, whenever I recollect my memories. Each and every second of my college life has been memorable so far. Though we had lots of misunderstandings and fights among us, we all were affable and had splendid days. I am really lucky to get such wonderful classmates as well friends.

Our 3rd semester batch missed the other half of our classmates. We just waited for our exams. At length, the day has arrived where we all could just see the rest of the classmates in exam halls, sitting with different question papers because they were rewriting their second semester backs. We felt ecstatic, the minute when we saw them back in college, though they were not in the same semester.

Yes, once our exams were over, we all were ready to get back to our hometowns, but before that we were very eager to know about our vacations. Finally, it's announced by the college management.

Chapter 4

After almost a month, it was college reopening day again. It was a beautiful morning where everyone in my batch was rushing to college prior to their usual times with lots of exhilaration as well merriment because each one in the batch were avidly waiting for a long time to see the whole batch together and it's going to be true that day.

It's really exquisite to see each one in my batch, as each one face carried a cute smile. And it seemed out one month semester holidays were too long because our north Indian classmates came back on the college reopening day itself and it never happened previously. Yes, the whole batch was chit chatting here and there in our department balcony except a very few, but my eyes were yet searching for Jack, by the time.

Suddenly we all could hear footsteps sound from the ground floor. I turned towards stairs immediately and my eyes were eagerly waiting to see Jack. Yes, Jack was climbing the stairs very fast with a few of our seniors.

Jack was wearing a yellow colour shirt which was nicely tucked into brownish pants. I was bowled over, when I saw Jack in yellow colour shirt because Jack always tries his maximum to avoid yellow colour shirts as yellow is my favorite colour.

Anyways, I was cheered to see Jack almost after a month vacation. Abruptly, when I turned back towards my classmates and friends, we all could see a few of our department professors were heading towards us.

We heard our new classroom allotments from our professors. Then my regular batch mates said; ok guys, let's split up, but don't worry, we would just put our bags in our classroom and we would come back to your classrooms. Yes, my classroom was very nice and each one occupied the desks according to their wish. Lalitha, Deepa & I sat together at a desk. Divakar, Prakash and Somesh together. Jack, Sobia and Meenu together in a desk.

Above all, the happiest moment was when I and Jack answered at the same time for a single question in our first session of 4th semester. The professor smiled at both of us and he asked me to tell the answer first, followed by Jack's answer there by classes continued. I was glad to see the Jack cute smile at me, during that class. We had splendid day's altogether. Though Jack was not speaking with me, his behavior towards me left me bemused again.

As usual, I started speaking mentally, why this Jack always leaves me dazed. If he doesn't love me, why does he behave like this? But, I had no answer. As days, flew by, on one fine day the heart beating moment happened when my professor picked Jack as a model for a practical session.

I was thrilled as well my regular batch mates as well friends chuckled when my professor picked me to demonstrate stretching exercises of the hand. The unforgettable comment from my regular batch mates as well friends was, Jack wants Deeksha to hold her hand a little more time and that's why Jack said; I could never feel the stretch. Otherwise, how come Jack will never feel it, when another model feels the same stretch in a few seconds when Deeksha demonstrates it? Then I remember thinking to myself; was their words true? If not, then why doesn't Jack feel the stretch, though I did it in the same way as how I did to other models? Awww!! Irritating!! Jack, how should I think about it man?!! Jack, you always leave me bemused.

Another heart beating moment happened within hours on the same day. Once the above practice session was over, we had one more session. The batch had been split into 3 groups and each group had one model. I wished my name should never fall into Jack group, but I was really stunned when my professor entered my name under Jack group. Also, I couldn't forget Jack's grin, when I practiced facial massage on Jack's face along with my other classmates.

By the time, I spoke mentally; This Deeksha will never ever come behind you Jack, until you accept your love for me. I am damn sure you will accept it because you love me more than I love you. It's never an infatuation and I hope you too knew it very well.

As days flew by, on one fine day, 2 of my friends of BDS batch just came to our classroom to meet my friend sayina during working hours. Unfortunately as it's almost end of a leisure hour of the day, they just came inside my classroom, sat with me and few of my class friends and started chit chatting with us for few seconds.

The next hour we are about to have our Exercise Therapy session but 10 more minutes had been left out for the session to get started. Unexpectedly, our Exercise Therapy professor came in just 10 minutes earlier for his session that day. So, they both left the classroom immediately. The professor asked; why the dental department (BDS) students are coming into this classroom during working hours and who asked these students to come here.

There was a pin drop silence in the classroom and no one opened their mouth to speak for a few minutes. Hence, the professor said he would never take a class for us until we guys accept it. So, whoever had done it, come to our department Staff room and tell me. Then only, I would come to your classroom, he said, and left for the department staff room.

At last, I and my friend sayina went, to the staff room. We met our Professor and said; those BDS students just came to meet both of us. The professor asked both of us to bring our parents to college the next day. Unless we bring them, we won't be allowed to attend his classes; he screamed at both of us. The next hour, once his sessions was over for the day, the professor came to us and asked both of us to meet our principal. We could meet her only after lunch, as its lunch hour. We were standing outside the principal room with tears rolling down our cheeks.

I could see my friends Lalitha and Deepa were coming downstairs, just to compromise me. I kept on sobbing and didn't have my lunch. Then, I was astounded when I saw Jack coming towards me with a wide smile on his face. I just saw Jack's face with tears rolling down my cheeks. Instantaneously Jack laughed at me and said; hey Deeksha!! For this small issue you are crying like a baby. C'mon, go and have your lunch first. Then you could come and meet our principal. Though I was astonished by his words, I have been yet crying and seeing Jack face like a kid, by the time.

Jack once again chortled at me and said; Deeksha please don't weep. Do you need a handkerchief to wipe your tears? Jack asked. Though I was quiet, Jack said; C'mon, take mine and then he gave his handkerchief. No! I don't need it Jack, I said. As I never eavesdrop to anyone words, including Jack.

As our afternoon sessions were about to start they all left back to the classroom. Then I met my principal. Even she agreed with our professor's words and asked us to bring our parents the next day to college. The next day, my father came down all the way to Bangalore from my native, and he met my Principal as well professors. Actually, my BDS friends came to meet my friend Sayina alone, but unfortunately they just came and spoke with me for a few minutes as its leisure hour and by the time our professor entered our classroom. But just to save my friend Sayina, I didn't say it out at that time, but as my father conveyed everything, I was left out with a single question by my professors. Why didn't you tell us very clearly that the dental students came to meet your friend Sayina. I just kept calm.

Anyways, going forward, try to speak away boldly Deeksha if in case you face certain situations, my professors said. Then my father left to hometown on the same day. I was happy, for 2 reasons. One was the issue got resolved, but the second reason left me bemused as usual and it's none other than Jack's.

When I recollected my yesterday's memories, I asked myself; though Jack didn't talk to me for a while, why did Jack come down to compromise me yesterday?! Who am I to Jack? None of my classmates or friends came to compromise me and Sobia, the exception was Lalitha and Deepika.

Another, bafflement was, why Jack asked me alone, not to sob? Even, Jack didn't speak with Sayina for a while, but why he doesn't compromise Sayina? She too was his friend right? But I never had answers for any of my questions. Then I remember thinking to myself; Jack, do you love me?? If not, then why you showed partiality between me and Sayina. Is it just an infatuation? No way!! Jack, don't you feel that this is love? Why don't you accept it? Do you want to leave me baffled always? Is that the reason Jack?

From next day, Jack was back to normal. It means Jack was not speaking with me as well with a few of our friends as like before. I felt, one of the hardest decisions we will ever make in life is choosing whether to walk away or stay back and keep trying harder. Then our batch semester exams were getting nearer.

We were terrified about our exams, as it's a break semester again. So, we started concentrating on our studies alone because our second semester (Break, Semester) results were blinking before our very eyes. During exam preparations each one of my classmates sat alone in a single desk in our leisure hours and started preparing for the exams. Then our semester exams started along with rain too.

It's really awesome to start our exams with nature showers. But we all never predicted that the nature showers would postpone half of our semester exams for more than a month. Yup! It's a beautiful morning where I couldn't believe my friend Divakar words through the phone. Our college management had announced leave for 1 month. Also, our semester exams were postponed due to heavy rain, Divakar said.

I didn't believe in Divakar words at the beginning. Divakar added; even I am going to my hometown. I will start today afternoon. Jack and Shanwar had also booked their train tickets. They would start today evening. Our semester exam dates and college reopening dates are not announced yet. College management would update us very soon regarding it. So Deeksha, start to your hometown, okay!!

More than that, you can stay happy because we have 1 more a month for our exams. Therefore, we can prepare well, especially for our practical exams. Anyways, I will call you later Deeksha, Take care, bye for now and then Divakar hung up. Yes, it's really ebullient to get holidays during our exam time. Hence, I went to my hometown gleefully. I thought I can prepare well for the exams again as well, I thanked the nature showers.

At long last, after one and half months the college had reopened. All my batch mates came down to college, exception was few north Indians. Our college campus looked a bit different due to heavy rain. Our postponed exam dates were not announced yet. We sat in a classroom and our Exercise Therapy professor entered our classroom within a few seconds. Then we had a random viva on Exercise Therapy subject, as the professor just wanted to check on our individual exam preparations.

In the mean time it seemed someone was about to enter the classroom and yes it's none other than Jack. Jack looked gorgeous with his favorite blue colour shirt which was tucked into brown colour pants. Jack said; excuse me, sir, my train was late. The Professor said; okay, Jack, come in. My eyes were looking at Jack alone until he sat at his desk. Then the questioner classes continued as usual. Our exam trepidation started again as it was break semester. More holidays made us forget all prepared portions, everyone said and that's true. Then, within a day or 2, our exam dates had been announced.

Finally, our theory exams were satisfactory and the fright able part was always the practical part. After a day of our theory exams, our practical exams continued. I was waiting outside my practical examination hall as it was my turn to enter the exam hall. The rest of my classmates were waiting in a classroom, which was next to the exam hall.

I was utterly jittery and was waiting outside. Jack and one of my classmates came out of the classroom and looked at the exam hall. And once Jack saw me edgy, he just came near me with his prepared notes and he gave his notes to me. Then Jack asked me to have a look at it, until I enter into the exam hall. Jack stood there with me for a few seconds and then Jack said; ok, you just carry on Deeksha, I would come back in another 5 minutes and he left back to the classroom.

Exactly after 5 minutes, Jack just came back and asked; do you want to read any other specific topic? Shall I bring the book Deeksha? Jack!! No need for it, I said. In between, we both could hear our external examiner calling my name twice. So I started rushing into the exam hall. It was a really horrible time I and my classmates had with our examiners especially external examiner. Somehow, the practical exams were over.

Next, we all started thinking about our results as it's a break semester. Anyways, as we had long holidays in between exams due to nature shower, we had college from the next day without semester vacations.

Chapter 5

Y es, it was new classroom, new expectations, though we all were petrified about our 4th semester results as it's a break semester. Apart from all those trepidation, we the whole batch had so much fun in the initial days of 5th semester as we never had classes for around 2 weeks. Then, as usual, our classes commenced.

We never concentrated much on it as we waited for our break semester results because we don't know what our kismet was going to be. On one fine day evening in college, we heard from a few of our seniors that our semester results were declared. The results were put up on the notice board outside the principal room, and it's not declared in our college website. After, hearing that, We all were tensed.

The whole department students, including our batch went downstairs near the notice board and started searching for our names. There was a big rush that we could not even see the board. I just stood behind a few of my seniors and juniors while checking my results. As soon as I checked my result, I could realize tears rolling down my cheeks automatically. I got 1 back. Then, gradually, I checked all my classmates' results.

My friend Prakash got back in the same paper as like me. Jack and my classmate Sobia got 2 backs. The rest of my regular batch mates had cleared and that made me feel low. The most scandalous part was the toppers of the batch had backlogs while the rest had done it. It brought tears into my eyes. It was the first time. I felt; This is unreal. This can't be happening to me. I wanted to pinch myself, to believe, it was a bad dream or something. So, I could wake up and it would all be over. But I knew it was all too real.

Before checking my results, I never ever felt, my destiny was going to be something different from my thoughts. However, destiny had something else in store for me. I couldn't even believe the results. I went back to my classroom, sat at my desk and dropped my head on my desk. I couldn't control my tears.

My tears were rolling down my cheeks continuously. As it was college, leaving hours, I just got up and when I was about to pack my college bag, I could hear my classmate Sobia crying sound, while Prakash sat at his desk with a sad face.

My whole batch mates don't know what they were supposed to do. In between all this, we heard Jack went ahead and shouted at the professors of our department. Jack had told our professors, the semester results were false, might be printing mistake. So, Jack asked our Professors to check back our results. We heard that one of our professors had also said; if Jack didn't clear no one should have cleared it, because Jack was one among the knowledgeable students of that batch. Then, what about rest 3 students, they were toppers of the regular batch right? I asked myself. Being a university topper, I myself have not cleared, then how could my professor say like regarding Jack's semester results. Sir Ji there are so many reasons left out to support your favorite student and not this way, I murmured. And one more bafflement was, Jack told his results might be modified with our classmate Rashmi's, as she was before Jack according to the attendance register number and the twist was she wrote all her 3rd semester carry over paper's along with her current 4th semester paper. College management was confounded by Jack's query. Hence, they said; we will check your batch semester results once again.

Next, our classmate Roopika was timorous about her results, thus Rashmi told everything to his father through the phone when she was in college. As Rashmi's father was a VIP in politics by the time.

Immediately, he came down to college with all media channels. Once the media person's entered our department, all our professor's rushed out of college, through our college back gates. The Professor's just waited in tea shops, which was located outside our college campus.

As it's college closing time and as none of my professor's were available in the department, by the time, the media person's stayed for more than half an hour in our college and then they left the place. Once media went out of college, we all could see 2 of our staffs gradually coming inside the college through the college back gate. Then our batch mates including me, started leaving for the day.

My friends Lalitha and Deepika accompanied me, till my room as I was howling incessantly. After reaching my room, I just burst into tears like anything. Till I am alive on this beautiful world, I will never forget that day of my life. Anyways, after some time, I slowly conveyed everything to my parents.

My parents told; you just go to college, let's see what happens tomorrow. Next day morning, before entering my department, I heard from a few of my classmate's that the semester results had been changed to Jack alone and for the rest it remains the same.

Moreover, I heard, the updated results were placed on notice board. We all, especially my friend Prakash, my classmate Sobia and I was stunned as well bemused after seeing those updated semester results in our department notice board. By the time, one of our junior professors, who crossed 3 of us said; these results are fake. So please affray for it. Being a junior professor, I won't be able to fray for you guys. Please never ever give up guys. You guys were eligible for 5th semester. We 3 just said; thank you sir. Then, the professor went to his class.

Next, we 3 decided to take the issue to our college chairman. My friend Prakash and my classmate Sobia were localities of Bangalore, but it would take one day for my parents, to reach Bangalore. So, we decided to meet our college chairman, the next day with our parents. The next day, once we met our college chairman in his office with our parents, we just conveyed our semester results issue.

We were thunderstruck, when our college chairman, said; he has not received any information about this issue yet. So, the college chairman asked us to wait for 3 more hours, so that he can speak with our department Principal, professors and then he would get back to us. At length, after 3 hours, when we met our Chairman again, he just asked us one question which left all 3 of us and our parents speechless.

The question was, did you guys have a photocopy of your old and updated 4th semester results. College Chairman added; I spoke with your department principal and the professor's. They said as follows; We pasted our students' semester results on notice board yesterday, after that we didn't update it. But they didn't answer me yet, when I asked why they didn't publish their department semester results as usual on our college website unlike all other departments.

Though we all had our mobiles in hand by the time, it didn't strike for any one of us to capture a photocopy of our results. Then, our college chairman, said; I always believe in our students' words. If we change your batch semester results again, it would be very obvious, that the results which had been published were false as it's already posted twice. So, for the 3ʳᵈ time, we can't change it.

Anyways, it's only 3 months left out for your next exams, as it's going to be a short semester. Therefore, you 3 just rewrite your backlog paper and I promise you, from now onwards, there won't be any break or carryover for each and every student of your batch. If you guys had come down to me, on the same day when your results were published, I could have helped you. But I'm really sorry guys as I can't help you now, but I promise nothing like this will happen in future. You guys can believe in your college chairman's words. After so much of problems nothing worked out. Hence, we just said thank you from our lips and came out of the college chairman's office with millions of queries in our heart.

We felt, being an average student, our classmate Rashmi cleared both break and carry over semester papers. But being class and university toppers, we were not able to make it. Then I remember thinking to myself, where does our knowledge gets rewarded? Money and position alone get rewarded everywhere.

Also, destiny is different from our wishes most of the times. Next, when we 3 came back to college instantly, we heard all our professors had resigned their job except a very few. Almost, after a week, we had so many new professors, new principal in our department along with a 3 countable old senior professor.

I never ever thought, I would lag behind from regular batch. But again, I felt that was my destiny. Those tough times made me to realize about all my friends and my classmates. My regular batch mates were ecstatic as well they all had 2 horns on each of their heads, which reminded them they all were super studious in their studies. And all my break batch mates were elated as well because even they experienced the same during our 2nd semester results. I always felt I had a wonderful batch, but at times when I think about this, my mind breaks my heart's trust which I had on this batch.

Next, Jack!! He never spoke a word to me after the results. I never expected that kind of attitude from Jack. And when things go wrong, we feel so dismal and all we wish for is to completely erase those bad memories.

Even, I wished the same by the time. I was surprised by my friend's Prakash words to me, on one fine day. It was an awesome sunset, where I sat with my books at my room balcony. I could see Prakash name flashing on my mobile.

Once I picked his call, Hey Deeksha, Prakash here. Yup! Prakash, I said. Study well Deeksha, Prakash said. My interest in studies had gone Prakash. I feel there is no value for subject knowledge at all. What's the point man, I said. Same here Deeksha, even I didn't touch my book until yesterday. Just now I opened my books, Prakash said.

I always thought either I or you should score top marks and it should be none other than us, Prakash added. Suddenly I remembered Prakash short term goal which he undertook at our graduation ceremony when I got university top in the first semester. Prakash didn't wish me yet, but he achieved his goal as well he proved his talent by scoring record breaking marks in the previous break semester. Then, I said; Prakash!! Did you know? You are a good competitor for me in studies. Really am happy to hear these words from you. I am so lucky to have a friend like you in my life. God has been kind to me Prakash. Anyways, I will do my best in upcoming exams, Prakash. And you too study good man, I added. Yup!! Sure Deeksha, bye and then, Prakash hung up.

Everyone feels pain in their lives. We can use it as an excuse not to be one or we can use it to become a better and stronger person. I was fallen under the second category. Yes, my pains made me a stronger person than before. We 3 stayed back with our break batch mates and rewrote our backlog papers while Jack and Rashmi went ahead without any break and wrote their 5th semester exams along with regular batch. After all, our semester exams were over.

We all had given our best in our exams. It was semester holidays, then. I was thinking what else would be my destiny. Slowly my semester holidays were over. I never had the heart to get back to college but I didn't have any other choice.

Chapter 6

At length the college had reopened. Once I stepped into my department, campus. It looked a bit awkward to me as well for Sobia and Prakash. We 3 sat with other half of our batch mates in the new classroom.

We, especially myself and Prakash felt; what was the point in being a class or university topper. Was everyone from our regular batch done their break semester exams in an excellent way? And did we 3 alone, from our batch had done our break semester exams worst? Was it? Yes, it seemed that way, because only we 3 from our regular batch were pushed back to our break batch. Anyways, we felt, it's our destiny and it can't be changed.

Next, I didn't hear even a single word of encouragement or consolidation from Jack yet. Hence, I never cared for Jack anymore. As usual for first 2 weeks, we never had any classes. Gradually, my whole batch entered into our fun world, forgetting all our destinies. We all started roaming here and there. As the days flew by, Sobia had become my closest friend among my batch.

Initially my friends Lalitha, Deepu and Sayina from my regular batch used to come to our classroom during lunch hours. Then, after a few months, during lunch timings I and Sobia used to join our regular batch in their classroom after finishing our lunch and have some fun. Sometimes it happened vice versa.

I always used to tease and play with one of my North Indian classmate Monashka. At times, for fun, Monashka used to take my college ID card, pens and hair bands few times and she would give it to Jack, because she knew very well, I won't speak with Jack. And Jack used to receive all my things without saying anything and he would keep it in his shirt or pant pockets.

While leaving back to my classroom, I would just get back to Jack and ask for all my belongings. Afterwards, he would give back all my things with a big smile on his face. Days went ahead like that. Finally, my department had been shifted to our new campus building.

The college management shifted the whole medical and paramedical departments to our new medical college building which was just 7 kilometers away from our old college campus. On day 1, after reaching our new campus by college bus, before allotting classrooms my whole batch that's regular and break batch were asked to sit together in the same classroom for almost half a day. If my whole batch were together, it wouldn't be there without the fun and chit chatting. So, everyone started having fun. I just sat along with my friends Lalitha and Deepu at the last desk of 2nd row. Jack sat just exactly a desk before.

Then, we i.e. I and Lalitha started chit chatting about other things. Suddenly, when I turned towards Jack, he just dropped down his head on his desk facing towards me and he was staring at me. For nearly 2 hours, Jack was just staring at me like a kid who just wants to say something. Once my friend Lalitha saw Jack staring at me, she asked; Jack!! What happened to you? Why you are staring at Deeksha. Nothing guys!! You guys continue your chat, Jack said.

Finally the classrooms had been allotted. The batches had been split up and everyone was avid to see their new classrooms and practical labs. Hence everyone dispatched. As days went by, my break batch was supposed to have a model exam, but it seemed the model exam was postponed.

Our subject in charge asked our class representative, to inform about it to our classmates. Instead of informing it, my class representative told; our subject in charge is busy with some other important work, so he gave the question papers to me and professor would be coming into the classroom at the end for collecting our answer sheets. Its' just 10.30am exactly now and you all should return back your answer sheets by 1.00pm. Thus, my class representative asked us to start writing our model exams. Then, he distributed the question papers to all my classmates and we too started writing our model exams.

It was only 15 minutes left behind, for our exams to get over. By the time, suddenly one of my juniors came and said; your class in charge professor asked this class representative to collect your model exam answer sheets and hand it over to him at the department staff room. Hence my class representative started collecting answer sheets from all, who had completed their exams.

We had one tough question and all my class toppers of that batch, started writing it as we had only 15 minutes left out. But I didn't touched that question yet as I didn't complete my previous one. All of a sudden, the representative collected everyone's answer sheets, and then when he came to me, 10 more minutes was left behind, so I won't give my answer sheet now, I said. But he just took my answer sheet and left to department staff room.

Tears started rolling down my cheeks, as I left out one question while all other toppers attended. Once our class representative came back to the classroom, he asked; hey Deeksha are you crying?! He added; it's just a fake test conducted by me and sir, won't correct those papers. Professor told he will give model exam dates later on. So don't cry Deeksha.

As already planned out, you were joining in today's outing with our batch mates, right? My class representative asked. As it was Saturday and as we had half a day college, we the whole batch planned to go out in the afternoon to a theme park exception was a very few classmates, which included Jack and Meenu.

I was hushed. Guys come, let us move to our regular batch classroom, the representative said. Gradually, all my batch mates started moving to our regular batch classroom, including myself and Sobia. I was sobbing yet, by the time. When I went and sat next to my friends Lalitha and Deepika in my regular batch classroom, I wiped my tears.

The moment Jack saw me wiping my tears; he was the first one to ask my class representative, hey what happened da?!! Why Deeksha was weeping. Representative cackled and said; don't worry, Jack. Nothing is serious. Then, my class representative said all those model exam stories which had happened in our classroom. Then, Jack and everyone grinned at me. Then, I spoke mentally, what happens to Jack if I sob.

All my friends were keeping quiet. But why did Jack alone ask my representative. Is it just friendship?! I came back to my senses instantly, when my class representative bellowed at me. It seemed, he was asking me for a long time, hey Deeksha are you coming for today outing with all our batch mates. Then, Yup!! Sure, I said with a wide smile on my face. Okay guys listen, once the college gets over, we all will move immediately, and we can have our lunch over there, a few of my classmates said and everyone agreed.

Our batch had an awesome time at theme park altogether with much fun. As days flew by, our college management announced the semester exam dates to both our regular and break batches as well as to the whole department. So everyone was busy with their exam preparations. At last, both my regular and break batch had our semester exams. Then, it's time for semester holidays. Yes, we got around one month holiday. We all were so happy to get back to our hometowns.

Chapter 7

Yes!! One month holiday went just like a week for me. I don't want to get back to college that hastily. But I had to. As usual, I was keen to see my whole batch especially my friends.

Once I reached my college, I could see my seniors and juniors roaming here and there as well conveying their New Year wishes. I entered my department with a wide smile on my face. Also, I was glad to see my batch mates and friends back.

Slowly, my eyes searched for Jack. But it looked like Jack was not back yet. After speaking with all my friends, batch mates and a few of my seniors and juniors, I just stood near my classroom balcony and enjoyed all the witty conversations of all students of the department. Everyone seemed ebullient. Then, I entered my classroom. And when I started speaking with one of my classmates, we both could see someone entering our classroom abruptly and it's none other than Jack.

As soon as I saw Jack, I was hushed. Jack came to me and wished me a happy new year. The moment Jack touched my palms to wish me, I could feel the softness of his palms and that made me recollect Jack words to me once. Jack mom won't allow him to do any work at home and that's why Jack's hands are always so soft. I too wished him back, but Jack was holding my hands yet by the time.

The minute when my other classmate who stood near us said; hey Jack happy New Year!! Jack left my hand instantly and wished her back. Afterwards, Jack went to his regular batch classroom. Though I was cheery, Jack again left me bemused. I asked myself; Unlike all other classmates, Why Jack didn't leave my hand suddenly after his wishes?! But I never had an answer for that. I sat at my desk, as it's time for our classes to start. Then, my new professor entered our classroom. We had an introduction session.

We all were having fun days again. In college, on one fine day, evening, my break batch heard, a big fight was going on between Jack and our classmate Tanishq in the regular batch classroom. Sooner or later, we all rushed into the regular batch classroom.

The minute we all entered that classroom, our classmate Tanishq gave a slap on Jack face and vice versa. Jack face was swollen and as its end of the day, few of my classmates started leaving for the day. Others stood just like that. We all were astounded as well taken aback by both of our classmate's attitude. Then, a very few of our classmates compromised both of them.

Lastly, Jack left for the day, along with Meenu. Then, while taking my bike, I saw Jack in the bike shed. Jack kept his college bag on his bike and he looked at his swollen cheeks in his bike mirror. By the time, Meenu was asking, do you need any medicine Jack? I didn't speak to Jack or Meenu. Then, I adjusted my bike mirrors and when I was about to leave, I saw Jack from my bike mirror.

Jack was looking at me alone, with his hands on swollen cheeks while Meenu was yelling at Jack, but Jack didn't listen to her at all. Jack's eyes were on me, until I started my bike. Abruptly Meenu turned towards him.

Next, she saw me. I just saw both of them in the mirror alone and I just left the place. I never want to speak with both Meenu and Jack, because they both never spoke a word to me yet regarding my break semester results, which had become a big tragedy once to me. I spoke mentally, why should I care for Jack? Who was he to me?

The next day, we had a big session from our college management regarding the above issue. Also, they warned Jack and our classmate Tanishq.

As the days flew by, we received a circular regarding college cultural for the whole university. Also, we got the list of programs and the participant lists were supposed to be provided within a week from each department. So, my entire batch started discussions regarding cultural events.

Almost all my classmates except a very few, decided to participate in that year cultural program because we all would be in final year during the next year cultural program, ie., break batch in 7th semester and regular batch would be doing their project work, as it would be their final semester. So, we won't be able to participate as a whole batch in the next year college cultural program. Hence, we all were about to participate in few drama's, dance programs and mimicries.

My whole gang girls participated in a dance, along with a few other girls of our batch including north Indian girls. We had few more dances, a few mimicries, a drama and an instrumentation program from our batch.

Each and every batch from my department was participating almost in all programs. So, my department had a big participant list. Then it's practice session. It was really funny and awesome moments. Slowly, after a few practice sessions, north Indians and my few other classmates said, they weren't interested anymore and they left in between. Then the left out participants were only from my gang and one of our classmates.

My friends Jack and Divakar were there with us during the dance practice sessions. Moreover the dance practice sessions with my whole gang were hilarious. At length, we got a choreographer through one of my cousin's friends. Then, after a few days, I got a severe muscle strain in my leg. It became difficult for me to walk by the time. Hence, I said; I am not participating anymore in dance.

Next day, I just went to watch the dance practice sessions and sat along with my friend Divakar. Jack came and sat next to me.

After a few minutes, Jack asked; what happened; why didn't you participate. Are you alright? Deeksha!! I just gave him a riled look and kept quiet. Though Jack gazed at me, Jack hasn't spoken with me after that. Lastly the practice session for that day was over and we all started leaving for the day.

As it's the weekend, they all planned to have a dance practice session in Meenu home. Hence I said, okay guys carry on, see you all after a week, as I was on leave. Instantaneously, my friend Sobia told, she won't go to Meenu home without me. Thus, after giving so much of a thought, at last I accepted to go to Meenu home along with Sobia. I and Sobia don't know the way to Meenu home. Jack knew the way and as he stayed nearby to my room, Jack said; he would come with us. Then, while leaving for the day, when I saw Jack in the bike shed, I said; I would call him the next day morning. Immediately, Jack said; hey, wait, just take down my mobile number Deeksha. Then, Jack asked me to give a missed call to his number; so that he can save my number. And I did the same. After that, Meenu was kidding Jack and I could see it through my bike mirror.

Meenu mimicried like me in a languid tone; I will call you tomorrow Jack. By the same token, Jack chuckled at her mimicry. Anyways, I just left for the day. Next day, when I was about to start from my room, I could see Jack number flashing on my mobile. Before picking up the Jack call, I remember thinking to myself, how pleasant, it's to receive Jack's call, after so many years. Also, I remembered how Jack used to call me, a few years back. Once, I picked the call, I could hear, hey Deeksha Jack here, where were you now, started from your room? I am about to start Jack. I will wait at the point where we have to pick up Sobia. I hope you know the point. Am I right Jack? Yup!! Deeksha, I could join you in another 15 minutes. Okay, see you then, bye, Jack.

Next, we both were waiting for Sobia for more than 15 minutes, but she didn't turn up yet. So, Jack parked his bike and went to a small shop which was nearby. By the time, certain thoughts started running in my mind, how delightful, it's to be with Jack after such a long time, but Jack didn't speak even a single word to me yet!! Even I didn't. But Jack was the one who never ever spoke to me even at my tough times.

Even a third person gave me a word of encouragement at those arduous times, but being a friend you never did it Jack. So, I am not a dim-witted to come and speak with you. Jack was back from the shop then as well Sobia turned up too. Hence we started. Then, we reached Meenu house in next 20 minutes.

As soon as we reached there, all my friends turned up there in another few minutes and the dance practice sessions started. I just went and sat near the laptop table in Meenu home. Then, gradually as well hesitatingly, Jack came and sat next to me. And within a few seconds, Jack asked; hey Deeksha why didn't you participate. What happened to you?! I gave out a furious look because the moment, I reached Meenu house, I heard the same question from Meenu. Before I could answer her, she said; Jack told me to ask you. Hence, I didn't answer Meenu.

Anyways, the dance practice session got over by evening and we all went back to our homes. After reaching my room, I was thinking, again and again, why Jack kept on asking, what happened to me?! Why does Jack alone care for me in such a way, though he didn't speak to me for a long while.

In which category I should take this to my heart. Friend? Does Jack mean it? Or more than a friend?! Jack just wanted to know about me, especially when I weep, when I am sad or not keeping well. I knew very well that Jack collected all the information about me for these past three years through our common friend Divakar, though Jack didn't speak with me. And I had seen it through my eyes. But I always wondered why Jack did that because Jack always said, he doesn't love me.

Moreover, Jack never spoke to me for more than years together, after my break semester tragedy. A boy, who is more than a friend, will do all these activities, but why did Jack do. As usual, Jack always leaves me bemused!! Next, I extended my leave for a week in college up to my model exams, as my muscle strain got worse than before. Then, I heard through my friend Sobia, my gang dance got rejected in selection panel of cultural events.

After all, the college cultural events commenced. I couldn't even walk properly by the time due to my worse muscle strain on my legs. But my friend Sobia forced me to come to college on the final day of college cultural program. Sobia came to my room and somehow we went by walk to college as my college was very nearby from my room.

We both could see a big crowd, once we entered our college campus and when we were almost near to the event stage, we could see Jack and Shanwar coming towards us. The minute they came near us, Sobia asked; did your programs got over? As they both participated in an instrument program. Yup!! It got over just 15 minutes back, Shanwar said. Oh is it!! Sobia said. Yup Sobia, they both said.

Anyways, we both want to watch the other programs of cultural event. Hence, bye both of you, Sobia said. Then we both went near the stage. As usual, Jack didn't even speak a word to me. Next, we enjoyed our cultural events with the whole university students.

Really, it was much fun to enjoy the program with the whole university students. Though the cultural events didn't get over as it's already 8.30Pm, we just left back to our homes. After a few days, our model exams started. We all were busy with exam preparations. At length, we got our study holidays too. So, the exam days were back. After exams, everyone started getting back to their hometowns gleefully, as we got one semester holidays.

The holidays went a little tedious for me. I didn't speak with any of my friends, as I am not too close with any of my friends, after my break semester results. Sobia was my only close friend, by the time. But I didn't even speak with her. I thought about my destiny. Before and initially after joining college, I never felt my destiny would be entirely different from my wishes. Also, I wondered about the rest of my destiny.

Chapter 8

At long last, the day had come where we all had to get back to college. Everyone came early to college from their usual times and the whole department was busy in chitchatting like as usual. I just stood serene with my friends for a few minutes in my classroom balcony. Then, within seconds, the classrooms were opened and we all got into the classroom.

The first day we had the as usual introductory sessions from our new professors. Next, we got an information from the college management, that's we all should come one hour prior to college time, because one of our main subject would be taken by a professor who was coming from an outside hospital. And my entire batch, that's both regular and break batches would attend that session together on every morning. We all were asked, to be there on time for the morning session.

Our batch already knew, the final year was going to be tough for both our regular and break batches. Yes, we all never had time to think about anything else, apart from our studies.

Everybody started preparing hardly from the beginning of the year and the regular batch was headed with their project work as well. I could see Jack in our morning sessions, but we never spoke with each other. I felt my career was really important to me apart from everything and that's my purpose of being in Bangalore. So, those days my concentration was only on my career. In between, our batch had a choice to study the acupuncture course as well.

From both batches, only very few classmates joined the course. I couldn't forget the minutes, when I received my Acupuncture course completion certificate. Also couldn't forget the way, Jack looked at me while receiving it. Also, we had the chance to learn manipulation techniques through a course in our college.

We had students from all the batches of my department to that course. Again, the students were split into groups for practical sessions and my name was under the group where Jack was a model.

During the practice sessions, I didn't practice the techniques on Jack, though he was the model. Hence, Meenu said; Jack please asks her to practice with you, this is about our studies and even Deeksha had paid money for the course. So, she has to learn the techniques, but Jack didn't open his mouth to speak. Therefore, I said; that's ok, don't worry, I won't complain about the model, but by tomorrow I would change my group Meenu. Then, I left the place. I was completely fed up with Jack attitude these days.

Anyways, I felt my career was more important than anything else, so I changed my group, from next day onward. By the time, I felt Jack was going to leave college without even speaking to me and destiny was going to be different. I always got irritated whenever Meenu and Jack speak with my friend Sobia, when we both were together. I used to leave that place, by the time without more ado.

As days went on, we had our model exams and I felt that was the last time, I am going to see Jack in my life, because the final semester exams were scheduled during the morning for our regular batch and evening for our break batch. After semester exams, our regular batch would be posted to hospitals of Bangalore for an Internship. So, I can't see Jack anymore in my life. I almost felt like howling and I was a bit concerned too. Above all, I felt, I should never go ahead and speak with jack, because if Jack feels the same, he would come and speak with me. So, after finishing my last model exam, I saw Jack in my college bike parking area but we both didn't speak. I felt how destiny had changed our lives.

Being a class and university topper, myself and my friend Prakash were in break batch, but the average students, including a very few toppers were there in regular batch. Anyhow, I just left home, after that. I concentrated on my studies alone. Finally the semester exams had come down and we had tough times during our practical exams. Somehow the exams were over and it was semester holidays for us. The long semester holidays went like the hours of a single day for me and I never had heart to step into college on reopening day because our regular batch had finished the course and they would be there in internship at hospitals, while the break batch had a single semester left out. I knew, I couldn't see Jack any more in my life. So, I controlled my tears and started walking into college. It looked a bit awkward to me, when I entered my department. I could never forget the days, we all spent together. I missed all my friends except Prakash, as he was with me in my break batch.

We had a lot of fun, especially when we all were together. I always remembered their presence in college. And, also the laughter that we shared, the dreams that we had. But those dreams changed with time and left a big hole in my heart. I spent hours sitting and staring at blank walls, running all our conversations through my head and recounting times the whole gang had spent together. I wondered if I could go back to that time. It's hard to let go of the past, when its witness to the best memories of our life. I knew they had moved on in their life. They had got some other friends better than me. But I still wished they cared for me.

Somehow the days flew by, as we all never had time to think about anything, because it's time to run behind our project work as well with our exam preparations and we had a very short time. Finally, our break batch had completed our project and we were in to exam preparations. Then, within 15 days we had completed our model exams.

Next we had study holidays. Sooner or later, the break batch had also completed our Bachelor course. We just had 10 days semester holidays, and then our internship program started. We all were exhilarated. Yes, then it was a different experience at various hospitals. Also, it's lovely to meet and work with students of different colleges from different places during our internship life.

Another thought which always ran in my mind by the time was, what I was going to do after my internship. Unfortunately, I met Jack and Meenu in a hospital during my internship, as those guys internship were over by the time and as they were about to leave abroad for their higher studies, they just came to meet the Physiotherapists of that hospital, just to bid bye to them. Then, they came and met our break batch mates.

Jack spoke with a few of our classmates. Jack added; we both were leaving to abroad by next week, to do our masters for one year. Anyhow, bye guys and all the very best, Jack and Meenu said and then they left from there.

Next, within few months,the fun and nice learning moments came to an end for our break batch too. Yes, we all had completed our internship program. I really felt blissful and divine to be with break batch. My contemplation was, if I was in regular batch I would not have elated. Also, I would not have got a chance to interact much with the rest of my batch. Above all, I would have missed a friend like Sobia for life time. I would not have known the value of Prakash friendship. I heard through my friend Shamili that Jack and Meenu had left abroad last week. They boarded the flight from New Delhi.

Before boarding the flight Meenu had spoken with our friend Shamili and she conveyed the information. So, it was true, Jack was out of my life. Why did it have to end like this? I don't know how you could do this to me Jack.

I really didn't deserve that. Just one more chance was all I asked for. Suddenly, tears rolled down my cheeks. And nothing could stop them from falling; Jack had left without saying a single word.

Then, I remember thinking to myself, might be a very fair and beautiful girl from a rich family would be Jack's anticipation. I had misunderstood him these many years. I realized the words, which someone once said; Love is never wrong, but a boy can be. Those words went straight into my heart. Just carry on with your life. Don't give up. You still have a long life ahead of you Deeksha, I said to myself.

I felt; why I should try holding on to the past, when the future can be so much better. At last, in the next few days my college life had come to an end. It was time to depart. It was really hard to bid bye to all my break batch mates, especially my friends.

Every decision we make, leads us down a different road. So, finally, I and my friend Sobia decided to do our post graduation in clinical research in one of a big university in Mumbai. Furthermore, I felt; nothing is permanent in life. May be my life can have a new turn. After all, it will have a happy ending. I thought, Jack's part was over in my life journey! But, he came in again and as usual, he left me confused forever.

Chapter 9

My first visit to Mumbai with my dad and my friend Sobia was memorable yet. The moments at my institute were awesome. We can't forget Adithya's brain washing moments to join their institute for post graduation. And Adithya's, first question to us was fresh in my memories yet. Adithya asked; is it your first visit to Mumbai? If yes! Then what made you to come to Mumbai? Yup! Exactly your institute and nothing else, I and my friend Sobia said with a wide grin on our faces.

Finally, we decided to join in the same institute for our post graduation. The first day at a new college with new faces in a new city was fabulous. And our first visit to hostel campus with our parents is fresh in my memories. Life looked entirely different at Mumbai for me and my friend Sobia. We never thought we would get such a good set of friends in our hostel. Really, we had awesome moments with our friends Abhinaya, Mridhulla, Vanshika and with a few others in Mumbai.

Post graduation classes were different. We had students with different talents and different backgrounds, from almost all the states of India in our batch. We all learnt so many things in life.

It was incredible moments, when I shared my contemplations about Jack, with my new but close hostel friends, when they asked about my marriage. After hearing it, even they were left baffled as like me. But, anyways get married soon, my friends said. Mumbai had almost changed me, but my friend Sobiha wanted to get back to Bangalore and she didn't like Mumbai. But it's really treasonable minutes at temples, shops, bus stops without knowing the local language of the city. Also, couldn't forget the minutes at internet centers with my friend Sobiha, just to ping Jack and to apply for jobs are fresh in my memories yet. Jack never replied back to my emails. But my friend Meenu did.

All of a sudden, after a few days, I could see Jack emails in my mail inbox which made me hassle-free. Hey Deeksha!! How are you? How is your new life in Mumbai, did you get settled into your new environment and etc., Jack had asked. I was cheered to hear all that from Jack. At same time, I remembered, I was the one, who first mailed him.

I realized Jack was not interested to continue my friendship, anymore. Above all, I felt, if my love of Jack was true, he would come to me on one day regardless of wherever I am. I and my friend Sobiha had a tough time during our post graduation, as the subjects were entirely different from our UG program. So, we both strived hard for our careers.

As the days flew by, we didn't feel it pass, we had our campus placements. 3 companies had already finished their placements and we both were not selected yet. I was fretting. I thought, what would happen if I didn't get placed in any of the campus interviews. At length, I got placed in a top MNC for Bangalore location.

My parents as well Sobiha parents were so happy for me, but Sobiha's father's words were fresh in my memories yet. He said; Congrats ma!! The company where you got placed is a big one which is vastly like a sea. Anyways! All the very best dear. Then, within a few seconds, my happiness, doubled as my friend Sobiha got placed in a CRO and she was also posted to Bangalore.

I thanked God for all his blessings on us. So, again a new and wonderful step of life was ahead for me. I was excited as well as astounded. I was asked to join immediately, after my final Post graduation exams. In between all this, I never received any mails either from Jack or Meenu. I never knew what was happening in Jack's life over there in New York. I heard through one of my UG college friends, that they had completed their masters and they both got jobs over there. I don't want to contact Jack anymore unless he himself mails me. If Jack, never need my love, let him be. I just want to concentrate on my career ahead alone by the time. Then, I had my final exams of post graduation.

Next, as usual, it's really hard to bid bye to all my close friends as well post graduation batch mates. Though we were only 60 students in the batch, we all felt, it's not possible to meet everyone again in life and most of the times, that's all our life journey is about. I had my exquisite days in Mumbai. I felt, I would be missing the city. Finally, I and my friend Sobiha boarded our Mumbai to Bangalore flight.

Chapter 10

Back to Bangalore, was like back to home for me. I was glad to be a part of MNC life. I never knew what kind of bombshell was waiting for me over there. All of a sudden, almost after one and half years, I could see my UG college friend Divakar number flashing on my mobile.

As soon as, I picked his call, I was amazed as well, elated, because Divakar got placed in the same company, where I was about to join but his joining date was 15 days behind mine. Congrats Divakar, I am really proud of you because you didn't make any graduation in this particular field but your talent made you too. Enough Deeksha!! Don't praise me too much, Divakar said. Then, I heard one my senior was already working there and Divakar would be joining his team, whereas I would be in a different deal.

Divakar added; Meenu and Jack were in India on a small vacation. Anyways, All the very best and meet you in the office shortly, bye Deeksha, Divakar said and then he hung up. My joining date was on Meenu birthday. So, I just tried to Meenu's home phone number by around 7 am to wish her for her birthday.

Someone received the phone and handed over it to Meenu. I conveyed my wishes to her, and then she invited me to her birthday party. Though I didn't ask anything about Jack, Meenu said, Jack only received your call. Oh!! Okay Meenu, anyhow, I am getting late to office, if possible I would meet you today evening, I said. I bid bye to her and hung up. Then, I remember thinking myself, Jack couldn't recognize my voice and vice versa. Anyways, I started to the office after that.

I was thrilled as everything looked new to me, but I had amazing minutes in my office. Lovely to meet so many new faces as well my awesome team. So overall it's a new and remarkable experience for me. At the end of day as I was exhausted, I just want to leave for the day. Yes, at last, I reached home almost by 8pm and I didn't call back Meenu.

The next day morning, when I tried calling meenu home, her father received it and he said, Jack and Meenu had already left to US by today morning flight. He added; I just now reached home from airport. That's okay!! Uncle. I couldn't make it to Meenu birthday party, as I got stuck in the office because it was my first day at the office. So, just let Meenu know, about it. Bye, uncle, I said and I hung up. Then, I started to the office. So, I was in the new atmosphere for 2nd day at my office.

I was excited as well a little hesitated. As the days flew by, I was glad to be part of such a wonderful team. I was delighted on the career path, I had chosen. It's really lovely to be a part of the research team. Then, I met my college friend Divakar and my college senior in office with their team. I never had contact with any of my college friends, an exception was Divakar. I had gotten very good friends for a lifetime in my office. As the days flew by, I started receiving marriage cards from all my college friends, one by one. I started receiving pressure from my home to get married.

My parents started seeing marriage proposals for me. I never knew, what I should say to my parents because I felt, I need my bachelor life for some more years and the reason behind it was I believed firmly Jack would come back to me very soon and say, I Love you and I want to marry you Deeksha.

By the time, I couldn't forget my college friend Prakash words to me, regarding my marriage. Jack was not a right choice for you

Deeksha, so please go ahead with arranged marriage, Prakash said. I felt, why I should not go ahead with arranged marriage because it seemed Jack was not going to turn up, but I didn't accept for any marriage proposal by the time.

As the days flew by, on one fine day, when I was there in social networking site, unexpectedly, I could see a chat popping up from Jack, hi, how are you Deeksha. I was stunned as well as astounded after seeing it, because Jack had replied twice or thrice for my emails during my Post Graduation in Mumbai.

Moreover, he had never spoken with me for more than years, that's after my UG break semester results which was a big tragedy once. I didn't reply back to Jack, for a few minutes, but I always never had a heart to hurt anyone. Though I didn't want to speak with Jack at that time, I replied back, saying hey Jack!! I am fine here. How are you and what's up!! I am back to India, as I had visa renewal problems. I am in my hometown New Delhi searching for job over here, Jack said. Oh is it?!!

Anyways, it's time for me to start to the office, I will get in touch with you later, Jack, bye, I said and hung up. From next day onward, whenever I was there on social networking sites, Jack used to come online. Then, slowly after a few seconds he used to start sending messages to me. I never liked it, at the beginning because but at the same time, I don't want to hurt him also. So, I started responding back to Jack's chat, but I used to end his chat as soon as possible.

By the time, I was beginning to understand what someone had once said; some love stories can never be predicted. As soon as the days flew by, I heard from Jack that he had a big fight with our friend Meenu. And it's almost four years by the time, Meenu didn't speak with Jack. I remembered, though they both know each other as a friend Jack always used to say, Meenu as his sister as she looks exactly like her cousin sister.

Additionally, they both were like family friends. I came back to my senses, when I saw Jack chat popping up on my computer screen.

Did you have contact with her, Jack asked. Yup!! Meenu came and invited me to her marriage last year. By the time, I didn't ask anything to her about you Jack, even Meenu didn't say anything. Meenu has a kid now and she was in London, I said. Oh!! Is it?! She didn't even invite me to her marriage, Jack said. I was surprised after hearing that word, from Jack; because they both were good siblings as well their families were so close. Above all, they were wonderful brother and sister. Then, I could hear from Jack, anyhow, it's her fault alone.

Meenu would realize it someday. I also knew she would be back at my sister, Jack added. I didn't react at all for that. I could still remember both Meenu and Jack's egoistic attitudes towards me from college days. So, I don't want to know about all their nonsense fights, regardless of whatever it might be. Next, Jack said; did you know one more thing Deeksha, because of Meenu; I had lost all your friendships.

Though I was hushed by the time, my face expands to have a cute smile on it, while certain thoughts started flowing in my mind and that was, at least, by that time, Jack had realized it. Also, I remembered my friend Lalitha words regarding Meenu. It's you, who introduced Jack to our Gang, especially to Meenu, but Meenu had taken Jack away from you. You couldn't realize it Deeksha because you were thinking everyone was so good, but trust me that's the reality, Lalitha said.

By the time, I felt, my friend Lalitha words to me once were true. Anyways, it's time for me to get ready for office; bye, Jack; I said and came out of the chat. Finally, I felt, I am not the same old Deeksha to sit and feel for Jack. It's Jack's life and not mine.

After those many years, even I started thinking, Jack words might be true!! What I had on Jack might be an infatuation. Jack was chatting with me daily, after that, for a few more months. But I started avoiding him, as much I can. My college friend Divakar said; Jack doesn't even think about us before leaving India as well when he was there in New York. At least did Jack speak with any of our friends, during his vacation in India?! No right?! Then, why did Jack want to speak with us now?! Deeksha, we all were not friends for Jack. Understood?!! So, don't speak with Jack. Even, I received a call from Jack, but I never picked up his call. I just kept quiet to Divakar Words.

However, my shift was over, bye Deeksha, see you tomorrow, Divakar said and he left for the day. Then, I left back to my cabin at the office. I realized, Divakar words were true, at the same time, I don't want to hurt Jack, as like my all other friends, by not talking with him.

As the days flew by, on one weary day, when I was getting back to home from office, I just dropped my head in my car back seat and closed my eyes. What a heavy work load at the office, I murmured to myself. Suddenly, my mobile was ringing and when I opened my eyes to see who it was. I was confounded as well astonished because Jack number was flashing on my mobile almost after 5 years. I was not interested to talk with him anymore, so, I didn't pick Jack call.

At the same time, as I don't want to hurt him, I messaged Jack instantly, saying I was on the way to home from office. That's the reason; I didn't pick your call. Oh!! Ok! Call me after reaching home, Jack replied. Then, I was thinking about my destiny and what it has in store for me. So, almost after one and half hours, I reached my room.

Once, I finished my as usual works, I just sat before television. I never called back Jack. It's almost 5.40 pm; again, I could see Jack number flashing on my mobile. I got irritated but I picked his call. Hey Deeksha, just come online, Jack said and he hung up. I felt, Jack won't leave me, if I didn't speak with him. So, I just went online through social networking site and I could see Jack was already there online.

Immediately, Jack messaged me. Hey Deeksha!! How are you? How was your day at office? Hope you are tired enough and am I disturbing you?!! I smiled and said, Yup!! Sure, I am tired enough.

Anyways, what's up? I was surprised when I saw your call Jack. Nothing!! I simply called you, Jack said. Though I become furious, after hearing that from jack, I remained hushed.

After a small pause, Jack started asking me; Deeksha can you explain your job nature. Then, where you want to settle down after marriage? Did you receive any marriage proposals?!! I really wondered why Jack asked all those questions to me, but I answered back Jack without raising any questions as well without any hesitation. Then, Jack said; he was trying for jobs in United Kingdom as well in India. After a small pause, Jack added, Deeksha my mom asked about you yesterday. I was shocked after hearing it. Why did your mom ask about me Jack?!! Jack was quiet for a few seconds.

Slowly, again, Jack asked; what type of marriage proposals you and your family were expecting?!! Suddenly, Jack asked; is it possible to love someone and to live with someone else. What about your first love Deeksha? I understood Jack's point then. Hence, I grinned and said, No one would forget their first love and it would be there in their heart till they die. So, is it possible to love someone and to marry someone else? And is it possible to spend our entire life happily with that married person, Jack asked.

Yes!! Regardless of our wishes, we should go ahead with life at times Jack, I said. So, when is your marriage Deeksha? Jack asked. I don't know Jack. When, is yours, Jack? First a job in hand, and then I would be thinking about the rest of things, Jack said. So, come to New Delhi, if possible with your parents Deeksha!! Jack said. No! Not now Jack!! So, when?!! Will you come after your marriage to New Delhi, with your husband?!! Jack said. Might be!! I said with a big smile on my face.

Again, Jack said, so, you would be getting settled in Bangalore or Mumbai right? Yup!! Jack, I said. After a small pause, Jack again said, hey Deeksha, most probably, I would get job at UK. Do your company has branch over there, Jack asked. Yup!! The company has, I said.

Gradually, after a few seconds, Jack added; was it possible for you to get a job in your UK branch? Might be, but it's not that easy, I said. Once I get a job over there, you just try to come there, Jack said. I just kept quiet for a few seconds, and then I said, let's see, first you get a job.

Anyways, it's getting late and I knew you were already tired, but please have your dinner and then go to bed Deeksha!! Bye. I would call you tomorrow, Jack said. Yup! Bye Jack, I said and logged out of social networking site. At the end of the day, after retiring to bed, I recollected all Jack's conversation in my mind.

Suddenly, I felt, love was back in my life. I was a little bewildered about where my life was going. Then, I felt, Jack attitude towards me from college days were just like that day, but finally Jack would say, the feeling which I had and have on him was just an infatuation and nothing else. So, there is no point in thinking about it. Hence, I slept off. After a few days, I heard from Jack, that he got a Physiotherapist job in one of the biggest private hospitals in New Delhi. So, Jack was blissful and even I was delighted for him.

Next, Jack spoke with me and asked about my daily schedule and my leisure hours, so that he could speak with me in my leisure hours. After that Jack used to chat with me, whenever he gets time, from his busy schedule. As days passed by, I could see the same old Jack, as how he was during our college days. I didn't speak with Jack, as like before because he might say again, it's just an infatuation.

As the months flew by, it's Diwali festival time. I was about to leave to my home town, the next day. After boarding my bus, the next day, night, I could see Jack number flashing on my mobile. Once I picked Jack call, hey Deeksha, I miss you, Jack said. Though I was surprised by Jack's words, I was hush by the time.

After a small pause, Jack asked; did you board your bus? Yup!! Just 5 minutes back, Jack. So, when you were coming back to Bangalore Deeksha. After a week's time, Jack, I said. I know, you won't text me, when you were at home. So, please text me, once you are back in Bangalore, Jack said. Yup, sure!! Jack. Anyways! Happy journey. Take care, bye Deeksha. And I would be missing you! Jack said and then, he hung up. Next, I was totally bamboozled about Jack words; I asked myself; does Jack love me? But I never had an answer to that. Anyhow, I had an awesome festival time at home with my family.

When I was back to Bangalore after a week's time, I never spoke with Jack. After a day or two, as usual Jack started speaking with me again. Then, it's, almost the end of the year. I was there in Bangalore during Christmas holidays. Jack spoke with me, on the day of Christmas.

Once I wished Jack, Jack said; it's freezing over here in New Delhi. I couldn't even open my mouth to speak with you. It's shivering. I was under my blanket and speaking with you. So, Deeksha if I have a small peg of wine, everything will be alright for this climate. I remembered a Jack promise to me, during our college first year, that Jack won't even drink occasionally thereafter for life time, as because I didn't want him to. I came back to my senses, after hearing the Jack strident tone, Deeksha! What do you say?! I kept quiet.

However, I would keep my promise to you, bye Deeksha Jack said and he hung up. Then, I started thinking, what would be there in Jack's mind regarding this Deeksha. Does he love me? If yes, then why didn't he accept it? What would be stopping him? Was it my religion or Jack's family or what?!! Then, what's the purpose of keeping my promise yet? I couldn't understand anything.

Again, Jack left me totally baffled. It was an awesome new year, with wishes from Jack on my birthday. It was the first time; Jack had wished me for my birthday. Though I know Jack for almost 9 years, he never wished me, because we both would have fought for unnecessary reasons during or just before my birthdays. So, I was surprised by Jack's birthday wishes. Jack said, I had a hesitation from the morning, and as I was posted in ICU for the week, I couldn't wish you in the morning.

Just now, I came out; wished you, even I didn't have my lunch yet. You made my day, I feel so special. I will remember this moment forever Jack, I said. So, crossed 7 donkey years right?! When is your marriage Deeksha?! Jack asked. Stories later!! Go and have your lunch first Jack. It's already 3 pm. Even, I am starting from home; once I reach Bangalore, I would call you back Jack. Okay!! Take care! Bye Deeksha Jack said and he hung up.

By the time, this Deeksha never knew that would be the last birthday wishes to me from Jack. Then, my parents asked who was on the phone. Its Jack dad, I said. Oh!! You both were speaking again!! Yup!! Dad & Momma. Jack was speaking with me for past few months.

Good to hear that, my parents said. Both Jack's and my parents knew everything from the beginning. Withal, they knew we both were good friends. Even, I heard through my friend Meenu that Jack mom asked him once, not to speak with me, but Jack had scolded his mom for that from home until he boarded his train, after his vacations. Also, Jack had told his mom that he would never get a friend like me, so I don't want to lose my friend at any cost. Anyhow, finally I boarded my bus and I was back to Bangalore. Jack didn't call me, as he was busy with work. Jack was posted to night shift for 3 weeks. So, Jack spoke with me twice, that sol. I started missing Jack very badly.

Slowly, that 3 weeks, made me to realize that I loved Jack yet and to the core. I realized, it was never an infatuation. The feeling which I had and have on Jack was pure love. Once, Jack spoke back to me after that 3 weeks, though I was busy with work in the office, I picked his call, just came out of my office cabin and I said; Jack I missed you to the core, in the past 3 weeks. Jack kept quiet. Even me too, Jack said and smiled. Deeksha, I am going out with my mom now, I would call you a bit later, Jack said by the time and he hung up. Then, I decided to convey my love to Jack on the same day, when he calls me back. So, I waited eagerly for his call.

It was an awesome evening, with a mild chill breeze and it's time to be under nature showers in Bangalore. I could hear thunderstorms. Also, I could see flashing lights in the sky. On top of that, it started raining and yes!! I could see Jack number, flashing on my mobile by that time. Once, I picked Jack's call, I could hear, hey, what's up Deeksha? It seems you were so happy, Jack said. Yup!! I am under the rain. Can I say one thing? Something's been on my mind ever since you started speaking to me again. I whispered. Yes, what's bothering you? Deeksha!! Jack asked.

Jack for another 15 minutes you should just listen to my words alone, I said. Sure boss!! Jack said. I started speaking in a slow mesmerized voice to Jack. Jack, I Love You!! There is something about you, which attracts me towards you and which makes me think of you every minute!! I want to give you all the happiness you want!! You are someone for whom I can give my life!! I just want to live with you until my last breathe!! I miss you badly. I feel, I just want to kiss your lips, now.

Moreover, the feeling which I have is never an infatuation; it's just pure love Jack. So, what do you say? Jack!! Do you love me?!! I just closed my eyes and waited for him to continue. Jack said; Deeksha, just get away from rain first. Go inside your room, don't play in the rain, it won't suit your health. So?!! Jack, I said. Yup!! Just give me some time, not more than 48 hours. I would get back to you!! And please, don't play in the rain again. Change your dresses, have some coffee, then relax yourself, Jack added; I have not reached home yet, still with mom. I would call you, after 2 days. I too miss you badly Deeksha, Jack said. Oh!! Is it?!! Jack.

However, I would be expecting a positive reply from you Jack. So, call me soon, I said. Bye, take care Deeksha Jack said and then he hung up.

Then, what happened Deeksha?!! Roopika asked. Jack would have accepted his love for you. Am I right?!! If, yes, where is Jack now? And when you guys are getting married? When is your marriage Deeksha? Roopika screamed in joy, but Roopika doesn't know destiny was entirely different from our wishes most of the time.

Deeksha was hushed for a few minutes and tears were rolling down her cheeks. Roopika was shocked as well afraid. Hey Deeksha!!

What happened?!! Did I ask something wrong? If you don't want to tell me, leave it, but please don't cry, Roopika said.

Almost after ten to fifteen minutes, Deeksha controlled herself and when she tried to answer Roopika, words were not coming out of her mouth. Hence Roopika said leave it, I am really sorry, no need to tell it, if it's hurting you. I can understand.

After a few minutes Deeksha wiped her tears and said no, nothing wrong in telling you about my destiny. Again, after a small pause, Deeksha said; Jack is no more in this world now. Jack was dead. Jack as usual spoke with me three times, the next day, though he was busy in his hospital Work. I felt his happiness, after my proposal, but Jack said he would reply me back exactly after 48 hours from the time of my proposal regarding the feeling which we both had on each other.

The next day, I didn't receive any call from Jack until evening, so I tried his mobile number and it's switched off. Hence, I just went to social networking site, just to check his online status, but I could just see the status on his social networking site saying RIP Jack, which was posted by his relatives. Then, I tried to his home number, I could hear someone else voice on the other side saying, Jack died in an accident, that day morning, while going to work. I couldn't even believe it yet.

Tears started rolling down my cheeks automatically. I had no idea, what Jack had gone through and how he landed in that situation. I never had heart to see him in his death bed. Hence, I didn't attend his final ceremony, while a few friends of my gang had attended it.

I realized, it only takes a second for a life to be altered forever, but I had a very few such friends in my life, who stood by me like a family during my darkest days. I just took a leave to the office for a week with a reason, I am not keeping well.

I have been just like a mad for a week. I felt, why did I love Jack? Why do I still think of him? When I know, Jack will never come back. May be Jack wasn't mine. Wondering why I exist? Why does my heart beat? When I had lost my love? Who was more important than this bloody heart? It was something I never thought would happen to me so early in life. I couldn't even believe the destiny. To accept death is tough. One needs disobliging valor to do so. Withal, accepting life with all its error, bias and belligerence is very much harder. Then, gradually, I realized the truth, that Jack was no more in this beautiful world.

I never thought my destiny would be that way around. I always felt, I would marry and live with him happily for a lifetime. All my wishes, interests, and expectations everything was dead along with Jack. To accept things as they are is never easy, but the moment I thought about my parents, I compromised myself and started to office.

After that, I felt, everything happens as a pre planned coincidence. I am not supposed to wonder where Jack was, but I can't help it at times, because I loved him. But I can't sob all my life. I had to find a way to move on. So, I started living my life, as per the destiny.

As my dad was a heart patient, almost after 6 months, I conveyed about Jack's death to my parents. As soon as they heard it, they were sad. So, to cheer them up, I said, anyways that was the destiny and we can't do anything about it dad and Momma. There's a reason behind every new person's entry in our life. We may not know it then, but one day we may figure out why. They may form you, they may even break you and Jack broke me, I said. Then, I wiped my tears and went to my room.

After that, there was not a time in the day when I wasn't thinking about him. And each time, I think of Jack, only one question awaits me. Where is Jack now? He has been buried but that's his body. Where is Jack's soul? After death does life really exist? Has Jack taken birth somewhere again?. Is rebirth possible? Logically, no! Else Death is really the end?! But there are so many things still unanswered. After Jack's death, I always used to see the sky and feel, Jack would see me from there.

Also at times, I feel, Jack is alive somewhere and I shall continue to do what I did for the last 3-4 years; not talk, think or speak about him. And, the minute when I realize the truth, tears roll down my cheeks and I couldn't control it. And yet, I remember Jack's words during our college days.

Jack always used to say, we should always go ahead with our destiny. So, whatever happens in our life, we should accept it. Yup!! That's true. I realized it, after Jack's death. But I still remember his last words to me on the phone. Jack said, hey Deeksha, I have few more patients to look over. So, if possible, I will call you after work or else by tomorrow morning. And Jack never called me yet and he won't, I said with my tears rolling down my cheeks. But, if I think about it practically, I was really taking my life to that end of the road from which there was no turning back.

I had gone through so much in my life. I had experienced my life and it was not easy for me to forget about it. We can easily erase such memories from our mind, but our heart doesn't allow it to.

Life on earth is just that short moment you spend with your loved ones Roopika. Then there was silence for a couple of minutes. Every dream has wings, some fly forever and some are torn young, Deeksha said. Deeksha stared at Roopika for a few seconds. Deeksha seemed lost. Though Deeksha was physically with Roopika, her mind was somewhere else. Deeksha, everyone has a bitter past. We all go through so much in life. We should not cry over past memories, but learn from them, Roopika said. Then, Deeksha wiped her tears and said; Yup!! That's true Roopika, but the times that go away in the blink of an eye are actually the times, which eventually get placed inside the safe of our most treasured memories.

A lot of great things have happened in my life. In every girl's life, there is a boy she'll never forget and vice versa, and in my life it's Jack. Happy endings do exist; it depends on where we end the story.

There is only one perfect someone for each one of us. My parents were searching for my perfect someone now. So, you heard my whole story Roopika.

Could you tell me, the feeling which I and Jack had was just an infatuation or love? It's pure love Deeksha. Yup!! You are right, Roopika. But again, Jack left me bemused forever right?! Before Jack could accept his love for me, Jack was dead. Above all, that was the destiny for my love story. Then, the bus conductor switched on the lights in the bus and said; those who want to get down at electronic city, please come out.

Anyways, nice meeting you Roopika ji!! Just give your contact number!! Yup, sure. Just give a missed call. Yes, given, check it!! Deeksha said. Yes!! I had given, just save my number Deeksha. Roopika said; Yup! Sure! You had shared me your life and now I am part of your life Deeksha!

Though it had been only more than twice a couple of hours since we met, our friendship seemed old. It was the most amazing day of my life. Really lovely to meet such a wonderful person as well I am lucky to have you as my friend Deeksha.

Immediately, Deeksha hugged Roopika and said thank you, bye, Roopika ji!! And please stay in touch Roopika, Deeksha added. We both exchanged our smiles. Then, Deeksha rushed towards the bus door, to go ahead with her destiny. Then, Roopika was back to her real life.

Being an author, I think, the feeling which Jack and Deeksha had was pure love. So, after reading this novel, what do you say?!! Is it love or just an infatuation?!!

Author biography

Devi Vinayagam was born in Tamilnadu, India.

She completed her education in Tamilnadu and Karnataka.

She has a degree in Physiotherapy from Dr.Mgr Educational and Research Institute, Chennai and has completed post graduation in clinical research from CREMA, Bangalore.

She worked with Multinational companies (MNC) as well with Clinical Research Organizations (CRO) across Chennai and Bangalore under the drug research domain.

Currently, she works in an Indian company under the medical domain in Chennai.

Her passion towards writing as well as her real life incidents inspired her to initiate her first novel.

Reach her directly at drdevipt@gmail.com

Twitter: www.twitter.com/Devi

Facebook fan page: www.facebook.com/devi-vinayagamfanpage